He didn't dare take even one step toward her.

She was already so near that he felt as if he could feel the electricity sparking between them. It would take so little to close the distance between them.

Her gaze locked with his, stealing his breath as he saw the flare of heat in her eyes and realized it wasn't all anger and determination. She felt the heat between them. Her gaze shifted from his eyes to his mouth. Her lips parted as if of their own will. He felt a pull stronger than all his determination and was too aware of the bed next to them. Too aware of this woman.

She'd pried open his closed heart in a way that felt more than dangerous. *You think you got your heart broken last time? This woman could very easily rip it out and stomp the life out of it—right before she drove out of town.*

She blinked and stepped back, either running from the need in his gaze or her own.

BIG SKY DECEPTION

New York Times Bestselling Author

B.J. DANIELS

HARLEQUIN
INTRIGUE

This book is dedicated to Barb Otteson—a wonderful neighbor
and talented quilter friend who has brightened so many of my
days! For years, we hardly saw each other in the neighborhood
because I was blocks away at my office writing books. So glad for
the mini quilt retreats where we have gotten to know each other
and shared stories—and always laughter.
This one is for you, neighbor!

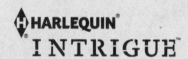

HARLEQUIN®
INTRIGUE™

Recycling programs
for this product may
not exist in your area.

ISBN-13: 978-1-335-59078-7

Big Sky Deception

Copyright © 2024 by Barbara Heinlein

For questions and comments about the quality of this book, please contact us
at CustomerService@Harlequin.com.

TM and ® are trademarks of Harlequin Enterprises ULC.

Harlequin Enterprises ULC
22 Adelaide St. West, 41st Floor
Toronto, Ontario M5H 4E3, Canada
www.Harlequin.com

Printed in U.S.A.

B.J. Daniels is a *New York Times* and *USA TODAY* bestselling author. She wrote her first book after a career as an award-winning newspaper journalist and author of thirty-seven published short stories. She lives in Montana with her husband, Parker, and three springer spaniels. When not writing, she quilts, boats and plays tennis. Contact her at bjdaniels.com, on Facebook or on Twitter @bjdanielsauthor.

Books by B.J. Daniels

Harlequin Intrigue

Silver Stars of Montana

Big Sky Deception

A Colt Brothers Investigation

Murder Gone Cold
Sticking to Her Guns
Set Up in the City
Her Brand of Justice
Dead Man's Hand

Cardwell Ranch: Montana Legacy

Steel Resolve
Iron Will
Ambush before Sunrise
Double Action Deputy
Trouble in Big Timber
Cold Case at Cardwell Ranch

Visit the Author Profile page at Harlequin.com.

CAST OF CHARACTERS

Molly Lockhart—She grew up believing her father preferred his dummy over her. On news of her father's murder, she went to Fortune Creek, Montana, to find Rowdy and destroy the dummy.

Sheriff Brandt Parker—The young law officer thought all he had was a murder to solve—and a ventriloquist's dummy to find. But it turned out that he and Molly had another mystery to solve—while trying not to fall in love.

Clay Wheaton—What was the ventriloquist doing lying murdered in a small-town Montana hotel? And why were so many people interested in his missing dummy, Rowdy the Rodeo Cowboy?

Georgia Eden—The insurance saleswoman has her own reasons for wanting Rowdy the Rodeo Cowboy found.

Jessica Woods—The parapsychologist/ghost hunter wants to check out the claim that Rowdy the Rodeo Cowboy was heard singing—after his ventriloquist was murdered.

Cecil Crandell—He did what he felt was best for his family—including sending away his son all those years ago.

Irma Crandell—Her regret—along with her anger—have been building for years. She can never forget what happened to her son, Seth—nor can she keep on pretending that she's forgiven.

Chapter One

Clay Wheaton flinched as he heard the heavy tread of footfalls ascending the fire escape stairs of the old Fortune Creek Hotel. His visitor moved slowly, purposefully, the climb to the fourth and top floor sounding like a death march.

His killer was coming.

He had no idea who he would come face-to-face with when he opened the door in a few minutes. But this had been a long time coming. Though it wasn't something a man looked forward to even at his advanced age.

He glanced over at Rowdy lying lifeless on the bed where he'd left him earlier. The sight of his lifelong companion nearly broke his heart. He rose and went to him, his hand moving almost of its own accord to slip into the back under the Western outfit for the controls.

Instantly, Rowdy came to life. His animated eyes flew open, his head turned, his mouth gaping as he looked around. "We could make a run for it," Rowdy said in the cowboy voice it had taken years to perfect. "It wouldn't be the first time we've had to vamoose. You do the running part. I'll do the singing part."

The dummy broke into an old Western classic and quickly stopped. "Or maybe not," Clay said as the lumbering footfalls ended at the top of the stairs and the exit door creaked open.

"Sorry, my old friend," Clay said in his own voice. "You need to go into your case. You don't want to see this."

"No," Rowdy cried. "We go down together like an old horse who can't quite make it home in a blizzard with his faithful rider. This can't be the end of the trail for us."

The footsteps stopped outside his hotel room door, followed swiftly by a single knock. "Sorry," Clay whispered, his voice breaking as he removed his hand, folded the dummy in half and lowered him gently into the special case with Rowdy's name and brand on it.

Rowdy the Rodeo Cowboy. The two of them had traveled the world, singing and joking, and sharing years and years together. Rowdy had become his best friend, his entire life after leaving too many burning bridges behind them. "Sorry, old friend," he whispered unable to look into Rowdy's carved wooden face, the paint faded, but the eyes still bright and lifelike. He closed the case with trembling fingers.

This knock was much louder. He heard the door

handle rattle. He'd been running for years, but now his reckoning was at hand. He pushed the case under the bed, straightened the bed cover over it and went to open the door.

Behind him he would have sworn he heard Rowdy moving in his case as if trying to get out, as if trying to save him. Old hotels and the noises they made? Or just his imagination?

Too late for regrets, he opened the door to his killer.

"MOLLY LOCKHART?" The voice on the phone was male, ringing with authority.

"Yes?" she said distractedly as she pulled her keyboard toward her, unconsciously lining it up with the edge of her desk as she continued to type. She had a report due before the meeting today at Henson and Powers, the financial institution where she worked as an analyst. She wouldn't have taken the call, but her assistant had said the caller was a lawman, the matter urgent, and had put it through.

"My name's Sheriff Brandt Parker from Fortune Creek, Montana. I found your name as the person to call. Do you know Clay Wheaton?"

Her fingers froze over the keys. "I'm sorry, what did you say? Just the last part please." She really didn't have time for this—whatever it was.

"Your name was found in the man's hotel room as the person to call."

"The person to call about what?"

The sheriff cleared his throat. "Do you know Clay Wheaton?"

"Yes." She said it with just enough vacillation that she heard the lawman cough. "He's my...father."

"Oh, I'm so sorry. I'm afraid I have bad news. Mr. Wheaton is dead." Another pause, then, "He's been murdered."

"Murdered?" she repeated. She'd known that she'd be getting a call one day that he had died. Given her father's age it was inevitable. He was close to sixty-five. But *murdered*? She couldn't imagine why anyone would want to murder him unless they'd seen his act.

"I hate to give you this kind of news over the phone," the sheriff said. "Is there someone there with you?"

"I'm fine, Sheriff," she said, realizing it was true. Her father had made his choice years ago when he'd left her and her mother to travel the world with—quite literally—a dummy. There was only one thing she wanted to know. "Where is Rowdy?"

The lawman sounded taken aback. "I beg your pardon?"

"My father's dummy. You do know Clay Wheaton is...was a ventriloquist, right?"

"Yes, his dummy. It wasn't found in his hotel room. I'm afraid it's missing."

"Missing?" She sighed heavily. "What did you say your name was again?"

"Sheriff Brandt Parker."

"And you are where?"

"Fortune Creek, Montana. I'm going to need to know who else I should notify."

"There is no one else. Just find Rowdy. I'm on my way there."

BRANDT HUNG UP and looked at the dispatcher. The sixtysomething Helen Graves was looking at him, one eyebrow tilted at the ceiling in question. "Okay," he said. "That was the strangest reaction I've ever had when telling someone that their father's been murdered."

"Maybe she's in shock."

"I don't think so. She wants me to find the dummy—not the killer—but the *dummy.*"

"Why?"

"I have no idea, but she's on her way here. I'll try the other number Clay Wheaton left." The deceased had left only two names and numbers on hotel stationery atop the bureau next to his bed with a note that said, *In case of emergency.* He put through the call, which turned out to be an insurance agency. "I'm calling for Georgia Eden."

"I'll connect you to the claims department."

"Georgia Eden," a young woman answered cheerfully with a slight southern accent.

Brandt introduced himself. "I'm calling on behalf of Clay Wheaton."

"What does he want now?" she asked impatiently.

"Are you a relative of his?"

"Good heavens, no. He's my client. What is this about? You said you're a sheriff? Is he in some kind of trouble?"

"He was murdered."

"Murdered?" He heard her sit up in her squeaky chair, her tone suddenly worried. "Where's Rowdy?"

What was it with this dummy? "I…don't know."

"Rowdy would have been with him. Clay never let him out of his sight. He took Rowdy everywhere with him. I doubt he went to the toilet without him. Are you telling me Rowdy is missing?"

Brandt ran a hand down over his face. He had to ask. "What is it with this dummy?"

"I beg your pardon?"

"I thought you might be more interested in your client's murder than his…doll."

Her words came out like thrown bricks. "That… *doll* as you call it, is insured for a very large amount of money."

"You're kidding."

"I would not kid about something like that since I'm the one who wrote the policy," Georgia said. "Where are you calling from?" He told her. "This could cost me more than my job if Rowdy isn't found. I'll be on the next plane."

"We don't have an airport," he said quickly.

She groaned. "Where is Fortune Creek, Montana?"

"In the middle of nowhere, actually at the end of a road in the mountains at the most northwest corner of the state," he said. "The closest airport is Kalispell. You'd have to rent a car from there."

"Great."

"If there is anything else I can do—"

"Just find that dummy."

"You mean that doll."

"Yes," she said sarcastically. "Find Rowdy, *please*. Otherwise… I'm dead."

Brandt hung up, shaking his head as he stood and reached for his Stetson. "Helen, if anyone comes looking for me, I'll be over at the hotel looking for a ventriloquist's dummy." She frowned in confusion. "Apparently, that's all anyone cares about. Meanwhile, I have a murder to solve."

As he headed out the door for the walk across the street to the hotel, he couldn't help being disturbed by the reactions he'd gotten to Clay Wheaton's death. He thought about the note the dead man had left and the only two numbers on it.

Had he suspected he might be murdered? Or traveling alone—except for his dummy—had he always left such a note just in case? After all, at sixty-two, he was no spring chicken, his grand-mother would have said.

Whatever the victim's thinking, how was it that both women had cared more about the dummy than the man behind it?

Maybe worse, both women were headed this way.

Chapter Two

The sheriff walked up the steps of the historic Fortune Creek Hotel onto the full-length porch across the front. It was a beautiful late March day in Montana. But while spring-like and sunny today, it would change in a heartbeat and start snowing again. He took in the all-wood edifice that had been built in the 1930s by a wealthy easterner who'd wanted a hunting lodge for his many friends. Since then, it had changed little structurally. A tall rather skinny building, it rose to four floors with only four large rooms per floor.

While the building had sat empty for a few years after changing owners several times, a local man had bought it and was now remodeling the rooms, starting on the fourth floor. Ash Hammond was determined to keep it open year-round—no easy feat in a town as small as Fortune Creek.

"'Morning, Ash," Brandt said as he pushed through the large front door. The former football star nodded from behind the reception desk. "Sorry about the inconvenience."

Ash, his own age of thirty-four, waved off the apology. "Just another day in small-town Montana." A good-looking dark-haired cowboy, Ash had left after high school to play college football as a quarterback at the University of Montana. He'd gone on to the NFL, playing for a few years before returning to town to buy the hotel. No one had been more surprised by that than Brandt who'd rodeoed at Montana State University before going into law enforcement.

Brandt had returned home after working in several large cities as a cop. He'd quickly tired of the rat race, missing the peace and quiet of Fortune Creek. He figured Ash had felt the same way. Leaving had made sense at the time. Coming back had made more sense. He'd come home to escape it all, but murder seemed to be the one thing he hadn't been able to get away from.

"Any idea who did it?" Ash asked quietly even though the lobby was empty.

The sheriff shook his head. Murder here was as rare as hen's teeth, which was another of his grandmother's sayings. "Anything you can tell me about Mr. Wheaton?"

"He checked in three days go, paying in cash for a week." Ash shrugged. "Only thing odd was the doll he had sitting on his arm. It talked more than he did."

"So you met Rowdy?"

"Was that its name? Kitty said when she went

up to clean his room, she'd heard two voices inside, but hadn't seen another person when she'd knocked and Wheaton had opened his door. Looked him up on the internet this morning. Seems he used to be a pretty famous ventriloquist. Played Vegas."

"So what was he doing in Fortune Creek?"

Again Ash shrugged.

Brandt thought of the two women he'd notified of the death earlier by phone. "Do you know what he did the three days he was here?" The sheriff had heard everyone in town talking about the man and his dummy, but he'd never seen the guy until he'd died.

"He didn't go out much," Ash was saying. "Hardly left his room. Didn't let Kitty in to clean it. I hardly ever saw him, but the few times I did he always had the dummy with him. Alice said he came down to the café a couple of times. He usually had his meals delivered. She said he had the dummy with him, and the dummy did his ordering for him. She thought he couldn't talk."

Brandt shook his head. "But the dummy definitely wasn't around when you found his body."

Ash shook his head. "I only stepped into the room to check for vitals, then I called you. I left the room, closed the door and didn't leave until you arrived, so no one could have taken it when I was there. Think the killer took it with him?"

"Looks that way. Did anyone visit him during those three days?"

"Not that I know of," Ash said. "At least they didn't come through the lobby. But they could have used the fire escape exit."

"Isn't that kept locked?"

"It's exit only, but when I came up to check Wheaton, I saw that someone had propped the door open with a book."

"A book?" the sheriff asked in surprise.

"An old paperback. *East of Eden*. Read that in school, don't you remember?"

Brandt ignored the question and asked one of his own. "Did you remove the book?"

Ash shook his head. "Like I said, I opened Clay Wheaton's door, stepped in to check on him and called you. When I looked at the exit door again while I was waiting for you, it was closed and the book was gone."

"So it's possible the killer was still in the hotel and exited when you were busy in Wheaton's room," he said. Had the killer brought the book to prop the door open, which would indicate the killer had used the fire escape before? Brandt thought of the books on the shelves down the hall from Clay Wheaton's room. "Do you know if the book could have come from the fourth-floor lounge area bookcase?"

"Could be. Guests are encouraged to take a book and leave a book, so I never know what's there."

The sheriff frowned in thought for a moment.

If the book had come from down the hall, then the killer hadn't used it to prop the door open—his accomplice had. "Who are your other guests?" He'd seen a sedan parked out front. Nothing went unnoticed in Fortune Creek.

"An older couple. Toby and Irene Thompson from North Carolina."

He made a mental note to ask them about the book, before returning his questioning to the dummy. "The killer could have taken the puppet or hidden it in the hotel planning to come back for it. What time does Kitty come in to clean the rooms?"

"Should be along soon. You want her to help look?"

Brandt nodded. "For the dummy and the book. Tell her not to touch either if she finds them."

"She just has 402 to clean until you release 401 once your investigation is done, so I'll tell her." Fortune Creek didn't get a lot of tourists except in the summer. Things would pick up come Memorial Day then die off again after Labor Day—except when ranch hands came into town to kick up their boots. Often they'd stay at the hotel until they sobered up. Unfortunately, what happened in Fortune Creek, seldom stayed in Fortune Creek.

Brandt thanked his friend and headed up the stairs. He found his deputy interviewing the only other hotel guests from last night—the elderly couple who'd been in the room closest to Clay Wheaton's.

"Here's the sheriff now," Deputy Jaden Montgomery said and motioned Brandt over. "These people have some information for you, Sheriff. They were in the room next to the exit and just across from Wheaton's."

"Why don't we go down the hall to the lounge," the sheriff suggested. The four rooms were divided by a small sitting area. Once they were all seated in the alcove, deep in the overstuffed chairs, he pulled out his notebook and pen and took down their names.

Toby and Irene Thompson were a cherub-cute couple, chubby pink cheeked, bright eyed and quite animated. They wore matching T-shirts. His read, She's My Sweet Potato and hers, I Yam.

"You saw something last night?" the sheriff asked hoping they did have some information that would help with the case.

"Not saw," said Toby. *"Heard."*

Irene nodded, eyes widening.

Toby continued, with Irene adding her two cents after him, giving Brandt the impression that they always finished each other's sentences. "We heard a loud thud."

"Like a body hitting the floor."

"Then nothing."

"We'd gone to bed," Irene said.

"I was already asleep. Doesn't take much to knock me out."

"I was reading, just dozing off when I heard singing." She shivered and hugged herself.

"Irene woke me up."

"The singing was chilling, so sad sounding."

"Melancholy," Toby agreed.

"Then this morning we found out that he'd been…" She lowered her voice. *"A ventriloquist."*

"It finally made sense, the other sounds we'd heard like there were two people over there in that room."

"Which was odd because we knew there was only an elderly gentleman," she said.

Brandt chuckled to himself—the couple, who he suspected were about the same age or older than Wheaton, referring to the deceased as an elderly gentleman. *Do we ever see ourselves as we really are?* he wondered. Doubtful, he thought and reined in his thoughts.

Toby was saying, "We'd seen him a couple of times."

"Only when the housekeeper knocked on his door," she said nodding.

"Did you see anyone go into his room other than the housekeeper?" the sheriff asked.

"He never let her in, just took his towels and thanked her," Irene said. "Seemed like a nice enough man."

"Did you hear anyone on the fire escape last night?"

Toby shook his head.

"He uses a CPAP to prevent snoring so wouldn't have heard anything. But I heard someone coming up the stairs and then a knock at the ventriloquist's door. The door opened—the person went in. But, before you ask, I didn't see any of the men who came up the fire escape stairs."

"There were more than one? Two?" She nodded, but didn't look sure. "There could have been three people."

Brandt rubbed his neck, wondering if he should take any of this seriously. "You could tell by the sound of their footfalls on the metal fire escape they were male? How can you be sure none were female?"

Irene again didn't look quite as sure now. "I heard one person coming up the stairs. The second person was following the first but not closely. I'd say the first was definitely a male, heavy footfalls. The second…" She considered. "Maybe a male who was sneaking up, same when he left much later after the first one. Either he came back or someone else did, both quietly. That exit door makes a kind of swishing sound when anyone enters or leaves."

"Wait," the sheriff said. "Let me get this straight. You heard two people for sure? Close to the same time? Like they were together? But possibly a third?" She nodded. He thought of the book still propping the door open when Ash had come up to check on Clay Wheaton. "Did you hear the door close both times?" She shook her head. "The last time someone left by way of the fire escape stairs, was it before the hotel owner came up to check on Mr. Wheaton or after?"

"After," Irene said empathically.

That could explain why the book was in the door when Ash came upstairs, but gone after he found Clay Wheaton dead. "Did either of you use the fire escape stairs?" They both shook their heads in unison. "Did you ever see a book that was used to keep the exit door from closing and locking from the outside?" Another no.

"Irene probably didn't hear the door close behind the last one because of the dummy singing," Toby suggested.

She shook her head. "The singing was much later after the thud we heard and after I heard the first person leave by way of the fire exit. I heard the second one go, and then I heard someone come up the stairs. Then the singing started. I'm not sure I heard the person leave after that."

Brandt's head had begun to ache as he tried to make sense of what the woman might—or might not—have heard. Flawed recall was a problem.

Irene heard one individual come up the fire escape, then another one, quieter. Both went back down the same way, the second one later than the first. Then who had come back up and why? Did that mean that one of the suspects had been hiding in the hotel? Had that person used the book to prop open the exit door so the killer could enter? But who had removed it while the deputy was in Clay Wheaton's room?

The sheriff had too many questions and few answers at this point. He had to nail down times, if possible. "Okay, about what time did you hear the thud?"

"Nine twenty-one."

He glanced up from his notebook. "How can you be that precise, Mr. Thompson?"

"Toby, please. I set the alarm on my phone and noticed the time."

"He is very precise," Irene said.

"I was an engineer."

"He built bridges, had to be precise. I quilt so I also have to be precise."

"Okay, what time did the singing start?" Brandt asked, fighting to keep a straight face since these two were a kick.

"Much later." Irene made a face.

"Nine fifty-two," Toby said. "I looked at my watch."

Brandt looked at Irene. "That was after the two of the visitors had left by way of the fire escape stairs? That's when the singing began?"

She nodded. "It was…haunting. Almost child-like."

"We knew we were never going to get any sleep with that singing."

"So Toby, you called down to the desk," Brandt said. That's when Ash had gone up to Clay Wheaton's room and found the man dead. "You're sure of the time?"

They both nodded, their expressions emphatic.

"Did you hear anyone come or go from the room during that time?" he asked.

"After the thud," Irene said. "Nothing until the singing started."

"Which is why we thought he was all right," Toby said.

"Neither of you went into Mr. Wheaton's room?" he asked. Both shook their heads. "Did either of you see his dummy, the doll he used for his act?" More adamant shakes of the heads.

Ash had stayed outside Wheaton's room until Brandt arrived with the coroner so no one had entered or left the room. "I appreciate your time and your help," he told the two witnesses, although he had no idea what to make of what they'd told him. They appeared to be very credible. So how did he explain what they'd thought they'd heard?

"Do you have the time of death?" Toby asked.

"Not yet." But Clay Wheaton had been wearing a smart watch. When he'd hit the floor, at 9:21 p.m., the watch had asked if he'd fallen. He hadn't responded. The watch, programmed to call for help, did so after asking a second time if he was okay and getting no answer. The 911 operator had called Brandt at 9:25 p.m. to notify him.

He'd then called the hotel, talked to Ash, who called upstairs at 9:30 p.m. A man answered the phone. Ash asked if everything was all right. The male guest indicated it was. Ash had said it had sounded as if the elderly male guest had been sleeping because his voice was different. It wasn't until he'd gotten the call from Toby Thompson about the singing disturbing their sleep that he went up to the room and found Clay Wheaton dead.

The times checked out. So how was it possible the couple had heard the dummy start singing at 9:52 p.m.—twenty-two minutes *after* the ventriloquist died? Someone had answered the phone in Clay Wheaton's room at 9:30 p.m. but it couldn't have been him. The singing started at 9:52 p.m. Brandt didn't have an answer for that.

He started to close his notebook when Toby said, "I went online this morning."

"After hearing that the gentleman was a ventriloquist," Irene said.

"We watched one of his shows." They both fell silent for a moment.

"It was the doll singing that we heard," Irene whispered and hugged herself.

"No doubt about it," Toby said.

"After he died, his puppet sang as if…in mourning." Irene's eyes filled.

"I'm sure there is a logical explanation," the sheriff said. The Thompsons seemed to be anxiously waiting for him to supply it. He closed his notebook. "The investigation into his death is only just beginning."

"Murder," Irene said.

"Yes," Brandt said and looked to where his deputy was standing, looking sheepish. There was no keeping a lid on any of this. The murder was more interesting because of what the victim did for a living. Add what these two swore they'd heard… "Thank you for your time. I hope this didn't spoil your visit here in Fortune Creek."

As he walked back down the hall, he noticed that the Thompsons' bags were packed. He wondered if they'd cut their visit short because of the murder. He hoped not. Ash could use all the guests he could get if he hoped to keep the hotel doors open.

DEPUTY JADEN MONTGOMERY watched the sheriff coming down the hall toward him, wondering what Brandt had made of the old couple's story. It had given him chills. Then again everything about this old hotel did that to him—not that he was about to admit it to Brandt.

But the case? He was fascinated by all of it. Murder was so rare here that when he'd become a deputy, he'd never thought he'd get a chance to be part of this kind of investigation. Add in a ventriloquist and a missing dummy; he couldn't have been more intrigued.

As they ducked under the crime scene tape and closed the door of room 401 behind them, the sheriff looked around the room and asked, "Still no sign of the dummy?"

Jaden shook his head. "I thoroughly searched the room after the crime techs out of Kalispell gave me the all-clear." The sheriff had called for a state forensics team last night. The techs had arrived before the sun came up. "The dummy's not here. Thought it might be in the man's suitcase, but I only found clothing."

There was a large stain on the carpet near the bed and a battered valise by the door, but otherwise, the room looked unoccupied. He watched the sheriff pull on gloves and check the closet and bureau drawers. Empty, just as Jaden had found. Clay Wheaton must have either packed to leave the next morning or he'd never unpacked.

The sheriff swore under his breath. "Unless the killer took the time to hide the dummy in the hotel…" That seemed improbable given what the Thompsons had told them. They would have heard the person going up and down the hall—let alone if they had used the elevator. It was more probable that the killer took the dummy with him when he left by way of the fire escape stairs.

"Could have been a woman," Jaden said. "Shot the way he was, a woman could have pulled the trigger. Would have had to have had a suppressor on the gun though. Don't see a lot of those."

The sheriff looked at him and smiled. "Seems you've given this some thought." He nodded. "Nothing looks out of place to you?"

"You bagged the note the man had left with the two names and numbers he'd left to call. But the pen he'd used and the rest of the hotel stationery are missing and I can't find Wheaton's keys for his pickup parked out back either—not counting the missing dummy."

"You're sure the crime techs didn't find them?"

"They wondered about the missing objects as well."

The sheriff's cell phone rang. Jaden stepped away, but he'd overheard the gist of the conversation right up to the curse that left Brandt's lips as he hung up. He guessed the news hadn't been good.

"We've got time of death," Brandt said.

Jaden had arrived at the crime scene right behind Brandt. He'd seen the body. He didn't need the coroner to tell him that the deceased had died brutally and no doubt quickly. A bullet to the back of the skull and into the brain would do that.

"9:21 p.m.," the sheriff said and shook his head. "Clay Wheaton had been unresponsive at 9:21 p.m. Coroner said he would have died instantly because of the angle of the gunshot. Yet someone answered the phone at 9:30 p.m. in this room and it wasn't Clay Wheaton."

Jaden glanced around the room. "Had to be the killer, but why stay so long in the room?" He felt Brandt's gaze on him. "Unless the killer was looking for the dummy and then the dummy started singing and he didn't know how to shut it up." He could feel the sheriff's gaze on him. "Clay Wheaton was the one who threw his voice *not* the dummy."

Jaden had to grin. "Then how is it possible that the couple across the hall heard the dummy singing after Clay was dead?"

The sheriff groaned. "Don't get me started."

"If the killer was also a ventriloquist, he would know how to throw his voice. Also the couple across the hallway swore it was Rowdy's voice they heard."

"The dummy wasn't singing after Wheaton died." The sheriff said it in a way that meant it was the last he wanted to hear anything different.

Jaden nodded. "Not singing."

Brandt gave him a warning look. "I don't want this foolhardy theory getting spread around."

"My lips are sealed."

"Really? So how did the Thompsons know it was a murder?"

"They're a smart couple," Jaden said. "Crime techs combing the room, the yellow tape on the door—I think they figured it out."

The sheriff looked contrite. "Sorry. You're right. I had hoped to keep the lid on this as long as possible."

"You forget where we live? In this part of Montana where nothing happens of much interest, even the birth of a calf is news." It wasn't quite that bad. But Fortune Creek was so small that little went unnoticed. Didn't help that everyone knew everyone else's business.

"The killer must have been looking for the dummy and that's why he was in the room so long," Brandt said. "Period."

Jaden didn't dare look at the sheriff, let alone mention the singing again. "Right. In theory, we find Rowdy, we find the killer."

"Maybe," Brandt said. "Also keep your eye out for an old paperback copy of *East of Eden*. It might have been discarded somewhere on the grounds. It was used to prop the door open on this floor's fire escape exit. Bag it for prints if you find it. Also, there's a couple of women on their way to Fortune Creek who are very interested in Rowdy's whereabouts. It won't take much to turn this case into a rodeo if we haven't found that dummy before they get here."

"I just heard that Kitty is on her way," the deputy said checking his phone.

"Good. Get her to help you search this hotel for that damned doll and if you discover that paperback just lying around—"

"Right, don't touch it. Bag it as possible evidence." Jaden smiled.

"I'm going to check Wheaton's pickup," Brandt said. "Strange his keys are also missing, but the pickup is still out there. The coroner said they weren't with the body either."

Had the killer taken them, and then changed his mind about taking the truck? Or had he wanted something from inside the vehicle? Or maybe to leave something in the pickup?

"Hopefully Rowdy's in the truck," Jaden suggested. "You need me to open it for you? I've got my slim jim in my rig."

"No, you stay here and help Kitty look for Rowdy," the sheriff said. "I can get into the pickup."

Chapter Three

Molly couldn't believe it took this long to rent a car—let alone how many hours she'd already been traveling since getting the news about her father. She'd taken the last flight out of New York City and after two stops, had spent a restless short night in an airport hotel in Kalispell. This morning she'd taken an Uber to the car rental agency since being informed of the distance she still had to travel. Now all she had to do was get the car and drive to Fortune Creek, wherever that was.

She was thinking that it might have been easier to buy a car, when the clerk at the rental desk finally found the car she'd ordered online from the hotel.

"How long do you want the car?" the clerk inquired.

"I don't know at this point. Make it a week. Can I extend it if I need it longer?"

"Yes, but you will be charged at a last-minute day rate."

Molly sighed, telling herself this shouldn't take

more than a week. "Fine, a week." She noticed another woman waiting. Auburn-haired, about her own age, the woman was dressed much like she was, suit, heels and clearly just as impatient.

"I would suggest a larger SUV," the clerk said. "This is Montana—our weather is unpredictable, but this time of year it can snow."

"You can't be serious." Clearly the woman was. "It's spring."

"In some places," the clerk said and laughed. "Just not Montana."

"Fine."

"Where are you headed?"

"Fortune Creek."

The clerk's eyebrows rose. "If you're going that far north, you definitely want the larger SUV. That's almost to the Canadian boarder."

Great. She sighed and looked over again at the woman waiting. She saw the surprise on her face as well—also her sudden interest.

"I'm sorry," the woman said as she approached. "Did you say Fortune Creek?"

Molly held her tongue for a moment. The woman didn't look like a journalist, but you could never tell. "Yes."

"That's where I'm going."

"What are the chances you're both going to Fortune Creek," the clerk said with a cheerful chuckle.

Yes, Molly thought. "Journalist?"

The attractive brunette laughed. Molly caught the hint of a southern drawl in her voice. "No, I'm an insurance agent, Georgia Eden."

"Molly Lockhart, financial analyst. What takes you to Fortune Creek, if you don't mind me asking?"

"One of my clients passed away."

"Really?" Molly said. How many people could have died in Fortune Creek recently? She had no idea. Was it possible her client was Clay Wheaton? She couldn't imagine him buying an insurance policy on himself. With a start, she realized who he would buy a policy for though. Her heart began to hammer wildly. "Let me guess. Your client is Clay Wheaton."

Georgia looked startled. "How did you—"

"And the policy isn't on Mr. Wheaton, but on Rowdy the Rodeo Cowboy."

The woman was more than startled now. "I'm sorry, how—"

"I'm Clay Wheaton's daughter."

"Oh, I'm so sorry for your loss."

"Don't be," Molly said. "My father and I have been estranged for years."

"Do you want the extra insurance?" the car rental clerk interrupted. "We recommend it since your insurance—"

"Sure, whatever," Molly said and signed the form the woman put in front of her.

"That could explain then why we're both going

to Fortune Creek. I didn't realize Clay had any family let alone a daughter," Georgia said.

"He had Rowdy," she said. "That's all he needed."

"Yes, he was quite attached," Georgia said and chuckled at her joke, but quickly sobered at her inappropriate choice of words.

Molly laughed but was unable to hide the bitterness in it. "Rowdy was like a son to him."

Georgia nodded sagely. "I never saw him without Rowdy. Is it true that Rowdy is missing?" Molly nodded and they both fell silent as Molly signed more forms and was finally given a key fob to the rental car. "I understand he was murdered."

"I have an alibi," Molly said flippantly. "I wasn't even in the state."

Georgia seemed startled at first, then realizing it was a joke, chuckled. "Clay was quite the character. Not father material I take it?"

"I guess not, unless you're a dummy."

The clerk explained where she could find her SUV and Molly started to roll her suitcase out to the rental lot as Georgia stepped up to the rental agency desk.

But Molly hadn't gone but a few feet when she turned back impulsively. "I've just rented the car for a week. I don't know how long I'll be staying, but since we're going to the same place for the same reason…"

Georgia seemed surprised. "I appreciate the

offer and would jump at it, but it shouldn't take you very long to handle your father's affairs. I might be forced to stay longer than a week. I can't leave until Rowdy is found. So it makes it difficult since we aren't going for the same reason."

"I suspect we *are* going for the exact same reason."

"Yes, but…"

"I could have handled my father's…affairs by phone. I've come all this way because of Rowdy as well."

"Of course. I can understand why he has sentimental value for you—"

Molly's laugh was the first real one she'd had since getting the call about her father's murder. "*Sentimental?* That old puppet is nothing more to me than a piece of wood with some metal and cowboy clothing."

Georgia's mouth opened and closed like Rowdy's did. "That old puppet you're referring to is insured for a whole lot of money."

Molly blinked. "I know my father thought Rowdy was priceless, but worth a whole lot of money? You have to be kidding."

The woman shook her head. "It's why I'm here. Rowdy *has* to be found. Once he is, I have a museum interested in purchasing him for a long-term exhibit, so if it's money you're—"

"I don't care what that dummy is worth," Molly said waving away even the thought. "I plan to chop that piece of wood into kindling," she supplied. "So how about that ride to Fortune Creek?"

THE SHERIFF USED his own lockout tool, a thin strip of spring steel, to open the older-model pickup. Newer cars had more technology built in and were harder to get into. The crime scene techs had gone to breakfast. He didn't want to wait for them. If the dummy was in the pickup, it would save him a lot of headaches—two in particular who could be arriving in Fortune Creek at any time.

He popped the lock, pulled on gloves and opened the pickup door. It groaned and he caught a familiar smell. Huckleberries.

For a moment, he stood frowning as the scent dissipated and he wondered if he'd only imagined it. A quick search of the pickup brought him no closer to finding Rowdy. The dummy wasn't here. Nor was there anything of interest in the glove box, or under or behind the seat.

The only thing he found was a takeout container that had been jammed in the passenger-side-door cubby. He took a photo before pulling it out, wondering who had put it there. Someone Clay had given a ride to? He bagged it and the plastic spoon sticking out of it for prints, again catching a whiff of huckleberries and noticing a dark smear on the small white box.

The sheriff smiled. If a piece of huckleberry pie had been in the box, he had his first lead.

Alice Weatherbee at the café made the best huckleberry pie in the county. But who had eaten it? He hoped the crime techs could get DNA off the plastic spoon. Whoever it was hadn't wanted to litter so had stuffed the container into the cubbyhole in the door? After bagging it, he put the evidence back.

Satisfied he wasn't going to find anything else of interest in the pickup, he locked the doors. Once the forensic team was finished, the truck would be stored down in Kalispell until the investigation was over. He'd let the crime techs take the evidence to the lab. The truck as well as the take-out box would be tested for prints and DNA. He felt as if he was making headway. If only he'd found the damned dummy.

From a spot in the woods on the side of the mountain overlooking town, gloved fingers tightened on the binoculars now trained on the young sheriff searching the ventriloquist's truck. Clay Wheaton was dead. The news had already rocked the town. Murder had a way of doing that. But the worry was the repercussions.

The young sheriff moved away from the ventriloquist's pickup, his cell phone pressed to his ear. Troubling was the evidence bag the lawman had been holding earlier. He had found something in the pickup?

A curse erupted in the pines, sending a bald

eagle airborne and making a squirrel chatter angrily from a bough overhead.

The gloved hands slowly lowered the binoculars. A foolish mistake had been made, but with luck it wouldn't amount to anything. It was always the little things that got missed. The little things that put a person behind bars.

But not this time. The only one who should have to pay was Clay Wheaton.

And now he had.

THE SHERIFF WAS at his office that late afternoon when the rental car pulled up out front. He saw a slim blonde climb out from behind the wheel. She wore a navy suit, white blouse and heels and a look of all business on her pretty face. The whole outfit serving as armor, as she headed for the door.

From the other side of the car, a woman also in a suit climbed out, removed a suitcase from the back of the SUV and headed across the street to the hotel.

A gust of spring air wafted in as the blonde entered the small sheriff's department building. It smelled of pine and water and fresh green grass. Even before she was close enough for him to see the intent in her blue eyes, he knew she must be the daughter of the deceased.

"I'm Molly Lockhart," she announced to Helen.

"I'm Sheriff Brandt Parker," he said behind her, making her turn to face him.

"Have you found my father's dummy yet?"

"Why don't you step into my office, Miss Lockhart."

"I assume that's a no," she said without moving. "Sheriff, I can't imagine that we have anything to talk about until Rowdy is found."

"That's not quite the case. We have murder to talk about. Please. My office."

She sighed and entered but didn't take a seat.

He followed, closing the door behind him before going behind his desk. As he sat down, he took her in. He doubted the woman had shed a tear for her father. "Sit down, Miss Lockhart. I'm in the middle of a murder investigation. I need to ask you a few questions if you can make the time."

MOLLY HEARD THE contempt in the sheriff's tone. She'd already seen it in his narrowed pale blue eyes as she'd looked around his tiny office from his Stetson hanging by the door to a photo of him riding a bronc on his desk. The cowboy didn't like her, and she resented being judged by this small-town sheriff. She didn't want to deal with any of this and found herself almost wishing that she had just taken care of it on the phone.

But then again, there was Rowdy. She'd always promised herself that one day that dummy would be at her mercy. She pulled out the plastic chair he offered, sitting rigidly, her purse in her lap. Furious that she'd been forced to come here and be judged, she also felt shame warm her face.

This sheriff thought she couldn't care less that her father had been murdered. He had no idea the years she'd hoped Clay Wheaton would someday want to be a father to her. Instead, she'd always been disappointed and hurt. Resentment and bitterness had formed a shell around her heart. It would take more than this cowboy's condescending judgment to crack it open.

The thought of how hardened she'd become because of her father brought tears of anger to her eyes. She hurriedly brushed them away. "You said you had questions?"

"I'm trying to solve your father's murder." His tone softened a little as he said, "Do you have any idea what he was doing in Fortune Creek?"

She shook her head. "My father and I haven't been in contact in years."

That seemed to stop him. "May I ask why?"

"You'd have to ask him. He left me and my mother when I was nine. All he took with him was Rowdy. Rowdy was his life, the son he never had. He had no interest in a daughter."

The sheriff leaned back in his chair, clearly taken aback. "I'm sorry."

"So am I. Sheriff, I'm only here to take care of arrangements for my father's cremation and to pick up Rowdy."

"Well, you're going to have to wait on both

counts until the investigation is completed and the dummy is found," he said. "I can't promise you Rowdy will be found." He held up his hand to stop her from replying. "We believe that the killer took Rowdy with him. So the sooner we find his killer, the sooner you might be able to get the dummy—if your father left it to you. Do you know if he left a will?"

She shook her head, alarmed. She'd never considered he might have left the dummy to someone else. "Without a will, wouldn't my father's possessions, including Rowdy, go to his next of kin?"

"I would assume so," he said, clearly irritated with her again since the dummy seemed to be the least of the man's worries. "Now do you want to help me find his killer or not?"

She straightened in the uncomfortable chair as a tense silence filled the small room. She couldn't help but wonder how many murders this sheriff had solved. He appeared to be about her age, maybe a little older. There was a confidence about him. He definitely spoke his mind. Under other circumstances, she would have admired that. Nor was he bad looking. Quite the opposite if you liked that rugged cowboy type. She did not.

He studied her, curiosity in his intense blue eyes, clearly planning to wait her out. She didn't like thinking about what he saw. His silent appraisal of her forced her to speak.

"Like I said, I have no idea what Clay was doing

here." It wasn't much of a town. A few buildings on a dead-end road back in the mountains, miles from anywhere. She couldn't imagine why anyone would live here, let alone why her father would have come here. But she could see that the sheriff wasn't going to let it go at that. "Was he scheduled for a performance?"

"Not that we're aware of."

"Did you find Rowdy's case, the one he traveled in?" she asked.

"No. Can you describe it?" He took notes as she described a metal case the size of a child's suitcase with the brand and Rowdy the Rodeo Cowboy printed on the sides. He looked up to ask, "The dummy had his own brand? Can you describe it?"

She silently questioned why that would be important just as she had with the case, but said, "The brand was burned into the side of the case under his name. I suppose I can describe it. I could probably draw it better."

He produced pen and paper, and shoved both across his desk to her. She noticed how clean his desktop was. Must not have a lot of crime. She also noticed his hands. Suntanned with numerous small scars. A working man's hands. She wondered how long he'd been sheriff.

She picked up the pen and began to draw. She was no artist, but finally satisfied that it was a close enough replica of the brand, she pushed the paper and pen back across his desk to him.

"A backward *C* with a small *r* inside it."

"The whole thing appears to be on a rocker, if that makes sense." She saw his expression change. "What?"

"There's a ranch not too far from here with that brand. You have any idea why your father would have chosen this particular brand?" She shook her head.

"This is at least a lead." He sounded extremely pleased. He even smiled, giving her a glimpse of the handsome rodeo cowboy that was much easier to take than an officious sheriff. Also, a lead meant that she wouldn't be here long. She couldn't help the relief she felt. Once she took care of Rowdy, she would be on her way back to New York City, back to her life.

She would finally put her father and his dummy behind her for good.

Chapter Four

Ash Hammond had been watching from the front window of the hotel. He saw the young blonde go into the sheriff's office while a young brunette got out of the passenger side of the SUV and walked across the street toward the hotel. As rare as murder was in Fortune Creek, two visitors who looked like these two women was even rarer.

No longer on a major two-lane paved highway, let alone the interstate, Fortune Creek saw few visitors aside from the tourist months of summer. If someone showed up in town with out of state license plates any other time of the year, it was a good bet that they were lost.

From what Ash could tell, these two women had come here intentionally so they had to be the two the sheriff had mentioned. They'd come about the murder. He tried to remember the last time he'd seen a woman in high heels crossing Main Street, let alone wearing a suit. Only the undertaker from Eureka, the closest town of any size, wore a suit.

Ash hurriedly left the window to take his place

behind the registration counter as she pushed open the door. She stopped just inside it to blink in the cool semidarkness of the hotel's lobby. He saw her gaze take in the Western decor, much of it original, before she made a beeline for him.

He straightened, aware of his T-shirt and jeans, not to mention his worn boots. All the other guests, there'd just been the three recently, were gone, having either died or checked out.

"Afternoon," he said as he saw her glance at the cubbyholes behind him and the keys attached to wooden burls large enough that guests seldom pocketed them—let alone forgot to return them. "What can I do for you?"

"I need a room?" she said as if it should be obvious since she was dragging a carry-on with wheels.

"For how long?"

"Possibly a week. Can I pay daily?"

"Suit yourself," he said as he stepped to the computer.

She glanced toward the stairs. "This is where Clay Wheaton was staying, right?"

"Only hotel in town. I'll need some form of identification and a credit card." A Wheaton family member? This one didn't seem like a grieving relative though. That left…journalist. It had been a long time since he'd had a microphone shoved into his face. He hadn't missed it and wasn't looking forward to it happening again.

She dug in her purse, pulled out two cards and passed them to him. Georgia Eden, a resident of Chicago. He looked up at her, wondering why he'd detected a southern accent. The credit card was in the same name.

No hint as to what she did for a living or why she was interested in Clay Wheaton and his dummy. It had been years since anything had happened in Fortune Creek to warrant ink in a newspaper, let alone airtime on television, but this murder could go national because of a missing dummy—if not the once-famous ventriloquist. On top of that, this woman looked as if she could be a television anchor with her long, burnished hair and shapely figure, not to mention her ready-for-her-close-up face. He supposed she could be someone famous.

Still it surprised him that there would be even this much interest in Wheaton's death. From what he could gather online, the man and his dummy had enjoyed fame, but that had been years ago. Then again, Clay Wheaton *had* been murdered. They say nothing improves character like death.

"You doin' a story on him?"

"No," she said quickly. "Has the entire hotel been searched for Rowdy?"

It took him a moment. *"The dummy?"* he asked, his gaze drawn from the computer screen to her in surprise.

"Yes, the dummy."

"Sheriff's department is still searching every room, though I doubt they'll find it since all the rooms were locked the night of the murder." He heard the sound of boots coming down the stairs. "The deputy must be finished. I hear him now."

As Deputy Jaden Montgomery descended the stairs, she looked at him so expectantly that Jaden stopped in midstep. For a moment, it almost looked like love at first sight—both of them frozen, eyes locked.

Then Georgia Eden broke the spell—if there had been one. "Well?" she asked.

The deputy blinked and came the rest of the way down the stairs to the lobby. "Beg your pardon, miss?"

"Tell me you found Rowdy."

"The doll?"

"Yes, the doll," she said, clearly getting exasperated. Jaden held up his hands in surrender, his look saying *take it easy*. Jaden broke wild horses and had a patient, easygoing way with them that people said was nothing short of amazing.

But it apparently didn't work on Georgia Eden. "Do you have any idea how hard it is to get to Fortune Creek, Montana, from pretty much anywhere in this country and that after flying from Chicago to Denver and sitting there for almost five hours, not even to mention the endless drive to get to this…town?"

"Yes, I am aware of that," Jaden said. "It's why I stay right here. It alleviates that problem."

She stared at him as if at a loss for words.

He grinned and introduced himself with that same easygoing tone of his. "Deputy Jaden Montgomery. Welcome to our little town. Now that you're here, I hope you'll enjoy your stay. It's a peaceful place where you can get the rest you obviously need." With that he touched the brim of his Stetson and gave Ash a nod before walking out the front door of the hotel.

She bristled at the deputy's words, seeming still at a loss for words herself as she watched him walk out of the hotel. Ash had to hide a smile as he returned her credit card and driver's license and handed her the key to room 403. "You might want to take the elevator since your room is on the top floor." He motioned to the ancient elevator.

"Don't have something closer to the ground floor?"

"Sorry, we're renovating. We started with the fourth floor because it has the best views."

She stared at him. "Views of *what*?"

"Our scenery. You know, mountains, trees, our famous big sky."

The woman shook her head as she grabbed the burl attached to the key and the handle on her luggage, and marched to the elevator. He watched her go until he heard the front door open again.

"What are you smiling about?" Ash demanded

as Jaden came back inside the hotel after Georgia Eden had disappeared into the elevator.

Jaden laughed. *"Who was that?"*

"Seems she's here looking for the ventriloquist's dummy." He gave the deputy a pointed look. "Don't be fooled by her looks. You definitely don't want to mess with that one."

Jaden chuckled and rubbed the back of his neck as the elevator rose to the fourth floor with a clank. "I don't know. I do like a challenge."

Ash shook his head. "You really need to get out of Fortune more often."

BRANDT SAW THAT Molly was surprised that the brand might be helpful. Not impressed that he'd recognized it, but surprised it meant anything. She obviously didn't have much faith in him.

Nor did she know what brands meant in the state of Montana. They were registered; people held on to the rights for years even after they sold their ranches. He had several old branding irons from his grandfather's place and still held the registration on several of the designs.

After he explained this to her, she said dismissively, "I doubt the brand means anything."

"Was your father raised on a ranch in Montana?"

"No, he was raised back east, Boston, I think he said."

"Yet his costume and the dummy's were Western attire. As I understand it, his show was Old West stories and classic Western songs about life on the ranch."

"My father was a phony—everything about him was fake."

He heard the acrimony again and could understand it to a point. Yet, he'd thought he'd seen some sentiment when she'd first sat down. Even if the man had left her, hurt her, she must feel something for him. He thought of his own father, wishing he was still alive.

"Lockhart? Married name?"

"It was originally Wheaton. I took my mother's maiden name when I left home."

He guessed that at some time she'd been close to her father. Otherwise, she wouldn't be this bitter. "Is there anything else you can tell me?"

She shook her head. "I know nothing about him since I haven't seen him in years."

He had to ask. "Did you ever see him perform?"

She looked away. "The first time he showed us Rowdy and performed, he was terrible. My mother and I laughed. I'm sure we hurt his feelings. Why he wanted to be a ventriloquist, I have no idea."

Brandt realized she hadn't answered his question, but he let it go. "I wondered about that myself when I heard what he did for a living. Not necessarily your father, but why anyone went into that line of work. My deputy said he thought it was a way for a person to say things he didn't either know how to say himself or was afraid to say."

She scoffed at that. "Sounds like an excuse to me."

He nodded, kind of agreeing with her. "I assume you're staying at the hotel across the street?" Past her, he could see the woman who'd been in the vehicle with her now headed this way.

"Since it appears to be the only place in town to stay."

"Right. You know that's where he was killed on the top floor. In case that's a problem."

"No problem," she said getting to her feet.

"I saw that you brought someone with you," he said as the other woman reached the sidewalk outside the office.

"Georgia Eden. She's here for the same reason I am. But you'll find out soon enough. Please let me know as soon as—"

"—I find Rowdy," he said finishing her sentence and making her actually smile. She had a pretty smile, but this one never reached her pretty blue eyes.

"Yes. Also, I need to know when my father's body will be released."

He nodded. "One more question. I have to ask. Where were you night before last around nine?"

She gave him an incredulous look. "At home in my apartment in New York City. I worked late at the office where there are witnesses and when you called yesterday morning, I was at my desk at work. I'm sure you're aware how many flights you have to take to even reach a town with an airport in this state, let alone a place where you can rent a car. That a good enough alibi for you?" She didn't wait for an answer as she started for the door.

"Are you really not interested at all as to who murdered him?" he asked of her retreating back-side.

She stopped at the door and turned slowly to look at him. "Only as far as Rowdy is concerned. I'm sure whoever killed my father had his reasons." With that Molly Wheaton Lockhart walked out and Georgia Eden walked in, the two women sharing nothing more than a nod, he noticed.

AFTER HIS VISIT with the insurance agent, Brandt looked up to find Helen in his doorway. "You're not going to want to see this," she said. He hadn't had a moment to catch his breath since he'd gotten the call last night that someone at the hotel wasn't responding after an apparent fall.

Earlier, he'd barely gotten Molly Lockhart out of his office before the other woman, an insurance agent named Georgia Eden, came through the door.

He was still shaking his head after his conversation with Ms. Eden. "What now?" he asked as Helen stepped around his desk and called up a video on his computer. He instantly recognized

Toby and Irene Thompson, the couple he'd met at the hotel this morning, doing a televised interview. "No," he said, knowing right away what he was about to see.

"It only gets worse," Helen said and left, closing his door after her.

He watched the interview, swearing under his breath. The guileless couple no doubt began telling people they met along their trip about their night in Fortune Creek. Not just about the murder, but what they called the eeriest thing they'd ever heard—the ventriloquist's dummy singing a good half hour after its operator had died. There was a grainy clip of Clay Wheaton with Rowdy, the dummy singing "Home on the Range." "Isn't the Fortune Creek Hotel already haunted?" the interviewer asked. "I thought I'd heard stories about strange goings-on."

The couple paled, saying they'd had no idea.

Oh, great, Ash was going to love this, Brandt thought as he switched off the interview. The last time a rumor about the hotel had gotten started, it brought all kinds of strange people to town wanting to see the ghosts—then getting angry when they didn't.

He rubbed a hand over his face, recalling his visit with Georgia Eden who had informed him that she'd written a million-dollar insurance policy on Rowdy.

"On a *puppet*?"

"A vent figure," she'd corrected. "Clearly you have no idea how much an original ventriloquist's dummy is worth. The most famous one, Charlie McCarthy, is in the Smithsonian. The *Smithsonian*. People are fascinated by them."

"Really? They kind of give me the creeps," he'd said. A mistake given her reaction. "I'm doing my best to find Rowdy and the man who killed Clay Wheaton," he'd assured her, hoping by his inflection that she realized the murder was more important to him. "It would help if you knew why Mr. Wheaton was in Fortune Creek."

She hadn't, but added, "Oh, but this might help. The man over at the hotel…"

"Ash Hammond?"

Georgia had shrugged. "As I was leaving, I heard him mention that Clay asked for room 401." She'd raised an eyebrow. "Apparently, Clay had stayed there before."

"That is interesting," Brandt had said. "Back to possible enemies… Was there someone who might have been jealous of him? Another ventriloquist possibly? Or someone he ridiculed in the audience at one of his shows? Someone with a grudge?" She hadn't known anyone.

"I really need Rowdy, Sheriff. I have a museum interested in him for an exhibit," she'd said.

"The Smithsonian?"

"No," she'd admitted. "But still it would be an

honor for this museum to display Rowdy and they are willing to pay handsomely."

"I have to ask," he'd said. "If Rowdy isn't found, does that mean you'll have to pay the million dollars?"

"Not me personally, but yes, my insurance company."

He'd seen that it would probably mean her losing her job, which would explain why she was so upset over the dummy. "Who gets that money?"

She'd hesitated. "Clay's beneficiary." Clearly, she hadn't wanted to say, so he'd merely waited until she'd finally said, "His daughter."

That had gotten his attention. "Molly Lockhart?" She'd nodded, looking uncomfortable. "Does she know that?" He couldn't help thinking about how adamant Molly had been about him finding Rowdy.

"I… I don't know," she'd admitted. "Possibly. Possibly not."

"Then I would think that if she did know, she wouldn't want Rowdy being found so she could collect the money."

"She says she has her own reasons for wanting Rowdy found that have nothing to do with money."

"Isn't that what she would say even if she was hoping he wouldn't turn up?" Brandt had asked. "I couldn't help but notice that the two of you arrived in town together. Had you known each other prior to this?"

"No, we met at the car rental agency. We traveled together as a matter of convenience."

"Because you both want the same thing... Rowdy," he'd said, seeing that she wasn't so sure about that now. "Did Miss Lockhart say why she was so anxious to get her hands on the dummy?"

"She says she wants to destroy it."

He'd raised a brow. "But if it is worth money—"

"Apparently she has issues with the dummy—and her father." Ms. Eden had gotten to her feet. "Please. Find Rowdy and let me know as soon as you do. I'll be staying at the hotel." With that she had gone, leaving him wondering who had the most to gain—or lose—by Clay Wheaton's death and Rowdy the Rodeo Cowboy's disappearance.

Chapter Five

Early that evening, Molly answered the knock on her hotel room, not surprised to find Georgia standing in the hallway. She'd heard the quick click of her heels earlier and surmised that she was staying in the room next door.

"It's been a long day. I need a drink," the underwriter said, making her smile. Earlier Georgia had been wearing a suit. She'd changed into a sweater, jeans and ankle boots.

"I saw a Mint Bar sign at the end of the street," Molly said. "Come on in while I change." She grabbed clothes out of her suitcase and disappeared into the large bathroom, leaving the door slightly ajar so they could talk. "I heard you wandering around the hotel earlier. Find anything interesting?"

"You mean like Rowdy?" Georgia called back as Molly heard her move to the window. "I didn't find him. Can you believe this so-called view? It's just mountains and trees as far as the eye can see and nothing else but sky. People actually come all this way out here for this?" Molly heard her move away from the window. "I wanted to see the room where Clay was staying, but the door is locked although the crime scene tape has been removed."

Molly pushed open the bathroom door. She'd changed into jeans and a top. After moving to her suitcase she found socks and the pair of sneakers she'd thrown in when she'd packed in a hurry. She sat down on the bed to put them on.

"He was in 401 at the end of the hall near the fire escape stairs," Georgia said still looking out the window. "He asked for that particular room next to the fire exit stairs, so he's been here before. You don't have any idea why?"

"For a fast getaway?" Molly only half joked about the room by the exit, wondering if her father had been strapped for funds and hadn't planned to pay his hotel bill when he left.

"Why would he come here?" Georgia asked after chuckling at Molly's joke.

"For the view?" She shook her head as she finished putting on her sneakers. "Your guess is as good as mine." She stood. "It does seem strange if it's true that he's been here before. Did you tell the sheriff?"

"He seemed interested." She thought about the brand, which the sheriff said matched a nearby ranch. Maybe he'd already figured out that Clay Wheaton had been here before.

"You're a regular Sherlock Holmes," Molly said as she grabbed her coat and they left the room.

"I like gathering facts, which is helpful in my business," Georgia said as Molly closed and locked hotel room 404's door. "For instance, ventriloquists are rather unique. There are less than four hundred professionals in the world."

Molly glanced over at her, surprised by her.

"Ventriloquism is apparently easy to learn," Georgia continued. "You can pick it up in a few weeks. The trick is learning to use your tongue to speak but not moving your mouth or face."

The hallway was dim with shadows that played on the carpet. Molly found herself trying to imagine her father here alone. Alone, except for Rowdy. Why here?

"I like facts. For instance," Georgia was saying. "Did you know that there are sixteen Mint Bars in Montana? I wondered what the mint part was about. Apparently as legend has it, the mint moniker was associated with the mining boom in Montana. Mind if we take the stairs?" she asked changing topics abruptly. "That elevator gives me the willies."

Molly agreed. "Everything about this place creeps me out."

"Well, there was a murder just down the hall." She chuckled. "Sorry, I keep forgetting he was your father."

"You're not the only one." As they reached the

stairs next to the elevator, she turned to look back at room 401. What had he been doing in this town, in this hotel, in that particular room? Like Georgia, she wanted inside the room, even though she knew Rowdy wasn't there.

She kept asking herself, who had her father been? Not that she thought she would find any clues here to answer that question or the one that haunted her most. Why had he left her and her mother all those years ago? Just as strange was why he'd left her number as one of the people to call should anything happen to him, she thought as they exited the hotel and she breathed in the cool mountain air.

After a short brisk walk, Georgia pushed open the door to the Mint Bar. The wooden front door was weathered and warped. It took the two of them to pull it open.

Once inside, Molly had to take a moment for her eyes to adjust to the dim darkness. The building, long and narrow like most of those in town, looked as if everything in it was original including the old metal ceiling tiles that had been painted red at one point.

To her surprise, Georgia seemed right at home as she made a beeline across the uneven wood floor for two empty stools at the end of the bar. Molly followed, noting the cracked vinyl chair covers, the scarred tabletops and a variety of different dark stains beneath her feet before she reached the bar. Rustic was the only polite word she could come up with to describe the decor.

Climbing up on a worn, wobbly Naugahyde stool that had been repaired with so much duct tape she could no longer discern its original color, she started to set her purse on the marred bar top but changed her mind. A couple of older men wearing Western attire were at the other end of the bar laughing with the gravelly voiced elderly bartender.

"You tell 'em, Betty!" one of the men called after her as she wandered down to Molly and Georgia's end of the counter. Molly marveled how women of a certain age often dyed their hair red. Her own mother had and her grandmother. She feared she might too at some point, though had to wonder about the motivation.

"What can I get ya?" Betty asked, her voice more like a low growl. A pair of dark brown eyes peered out from a fallen lock of dyed red hair.

"I'll take a cosmopolitan," Molly said.

"Not likely," Betty shot back.

Molly glanced at the bottles of alcohol behind the bar. "How about a margarita?"

The bartender made a dismissive sound and looked over at Georgia.

"We'll take two bourbons on the rocks."

Betty smiled. "I like you," she said to Georgia and gave Molly the side-eye as she went to make their drinks.

"Seriously?" Molly whispered to her companion. "What is this place?"

Georgia shrugged and leaned her elbows on the questionably clean bar. "The end of the earth?"

"I'm sorry, but why do you seem so comfortable here?"

"Grew up in towns like this, bars like this." She shrugged. "Reminds me of home."

Molly studied her in surprise. "Home?"

"West Texas."

"You don't have much of an accent."

"I would if I got around my family—I'd pick it right back up."

Molly realized she knew nothing about this woman she'd offered a ride to so quickly as Betty brought their drinks. She took a sip. It wasn't that bad for well liquor.

Georgia saw her expression and laughed. "You should be glad I didn't order you a tanglefoot."

"I'm almost afraid to ask," Molly said.

"Don't."

"Got it," she answered laughing as she took another sip of her drink. She felt the alcohol go to work since she hardly ever imbibed. "How did you get into the insurance business?"

Georgia shrugged. "Straight out of a two-year college, I was offered a job. Just that simple. I kept moving up in the company until I ended up in Chicago. I thought I had it made." She took a gulp of her drink. "Now I could be starting all over."

Molly could hear the pain in the woman's voice. "What happens if Rowdy doesn't turn up?"

Georgia drew a finger across her throat then turned on her stool to face her. "You really don't know what happened to Rowdy?"

She shook her head, surprised by the question. "I haven't seen my father in years—let alone his dummy."

"You wouldn't destroy it, would you?"

"I would—I will," she said picking up her drink rather than looking at her companion. "Let's just say Rowdy has been a thorn in my side most of my life. Hard to admit that my father preferred a dummy over his own daughter, but," she said raising her glass, "he did."

"I'm not sure that's entirely true," Georgia observed as if choosing her words carefully. Molly finally looked over at her and frowned in question. "You really don't know?"

"Know what?" Molly said, thinking how little she knew about her father during his life, let alone his death.

"The insurance policy on Rowdy? Your father made you the beneficiary."

Earlier she'd thought he might have thought of her and her mother all those years ago and taken out a life insurance policy. "If he was thinking of me, he would have purchased an insurance policy on himself."

Georgia shook her head. "You were right the first time. He only insured Rowdy."

"Of course, he did and here I was hoping he might have thought of me and my mother."

"Is your mother still—"

"No, she died almost ten years ago."

"Did your father—"

"Know? I doubt it. It wasn't like he stayed in touch more than a few phone calls now and then as I was growing up."

"Well, he hadn't forgotten you," Georgia said, and apparently seeing how unimpressed Molly was, added, "What if I told you that if Rowdy isn't found, you get a million dollars?"

Molly stared at her. When Georgia had said that her father had insured the dummy, she'd never thought... She let out a laugh. "He valued Rowdy at a million dollars? Why am I not surprised?"

"It was the most my company would ensure the vent figure for," Georgia said. "But the point is, he made you his beneficiary so if anything happened to Rowdy... He was thinking of you."

"That makes no sense at all," Molly snapped. She was starting to feel the alcohol. Betty poured on the heavy side. "If he cared about me, he would have insured himself."

"He wasn't worth a million dollars," Georgia said bluntly.

"But Rowdy is?" She took another drink.

"He couldn't have known that he was going to

be murdered and that the murderer would take the dummy," Georgia argued. "Unless…"

Molly saw the glint in the woman's eyes. "Wait, you can't think that he planned this whole thing?" Another shrug. "That's delusional."

"Maybe he was desperate. Wanted to make it up to you with one grand gesture. Hired someone to kill him and take Rowdy so the insurance company would have to pay you."

Molly finished her drink. She couldn't believe this. Of course he would insure Rowdy. But a million dollars? The thought made her even angrier at him and especially Rowdy. "It's just a dummy," she mumbled under her breath.

They drank in silence for a few minutes. Molly started to order them another, but Georgia stopped her. "I'll have a shot of tequila."

Her new friend grinned making her laugh. "You got it, sister."

After they'd downed their shot chased with salt and a slice of lime, Molly coughed for a few moments, then laughed. "Maybe you're right," she said. "I did wonder why anyone would want to kill him—let alone take Rowdy. Can't you save your job if you can prove that he set this whole thing up?"

"Maybe," Georgia said. "I just hope you weren't in on it with him."

"Are you serious?" she demanded. Just when she thought they were becoming friends and that staying here until Rowdy was found wouldn't be so awful. "I don't need or want the money. I haven't been in contact with my father for years and I—" She stopped herself. "Why am I defending myself?"

Opening her purse, she pulled out a twenty and threw it on the bar. "I know you're desperate to keep your job, but I had nothing to do with any of this." With that she stormed out, her mind whirling, the alcohol warming her blood and making her feel lighter on her feet.

Everything had seemed so simple when she'd first heard about her father's death. Someone had murdered him and taken Rowdy. Law enforcement would find his killer and get the dummy back. She hadn't even thought about what she would do with her father's ashes once she had him cremated. Her only thought was destroying that damned dummy.

She'd seen how appalled the sheriff had been when she'd shown no interest in helping find Clay Wheaton's murderer. All she'd cared about was Rowdy—but not in the way anyone would understand how she could hate an inanimate object. They would have had to grow up in its shadow.

Now Georgia had her wondering if Clay had planned his own murder and Rowdy's disappearance so she would get a million dollars. Had he really thought she would want that? Who would do something like that? All to leave the daughter who he'd never had any interest in money? It made no sense.

By the time she reached the entrance to the hotel, she'd convinced herself that Clay Wheaton's death had been a random murder and the murderer had taken Rowdy thinking it might be worth money or just for the heck of it. By now Rowdy could be in a dumpster somewhere.

As she started to push open the hotel door, it was flung open as Sheriff Brandt Parker came out.

"I was just looking for you," he said. "Want to take a ride?"

He didn't seem to notice that she swayed a little and probably smelled like eighty-proof. Nor that a ride was the last thing she wanted after a day of traveling. But he was the law and he was actively looking for Rowdy—as well as her father's murderer.

"Give me a minute to freshen up and I'll be right with you," she said as she headed for the elevator, knowing she wasn't up for the stairs.

Chapter Six

The Crandell Ranch was next to the Canadian border some miles from Fortune Creek. Brandt didn't mind the drive on such a beautiful afternoon. Clouds drifted in an endless deepening blue in stark contrast to the deep lush green of the pines. The breeze was cool. In Montana there was often the promise of snow in the mountains. He remembered one Fourth of July when they'd had a snowball fight in downtown Fortune Creek.

He glanced over at the woman next to him. She'd made it clear that going to the Crandell Ranch to follow up on the brand was a waste of time.

"I really doubt Rowdy's brand has anything to do with a real ranch," she'd argued when he told her where they were headed. "Nothing about Clay Wheaton was real. He made it all up. He wasn't the man you seem to think he was."

He thought she might be right. But he couldn't quit thinking about the brand Molly said was on Rowdy the Rodeo Cowboy's case. Maybe Clay

Wheaton had picked the brand out of thin air. Or maybe he had a good reason for choosing the Crandell Ranch brand. The same way he'd chosen the Fortune Creek Hotel in Fortune Creek, Montana. The fact that Clay had been killed here and might have stayed at the hotel in the past made Brandt think the ventriloquist had some connection to this area. That connection could be the Crandell Ranch.

As he drove, he pointed out mountains by name, told stories about hard winters, strange things that had happened like the moose getting stuck in the creek and how it had taken most of the residents of Fortune Creek to get her out. Molly made the appropriate responses, but he could tell her mind was elsewhere.

"Want to tell me about it?" he finally asked. She glanced over at him in surprise as if she'd forgotten he was there. He didn't take offense. If anything, he appreciated that she didn't seem in the least enamored by the romantic myth of the cowboy, maybe especially the cowboy sheriff. Her father had destroyed that Western fantasy for her.

He wondered if she thought of him as playing the role of the cowboy sheriff, like in the movies where even outlaws were given a silver star if bad guys were coming to town.

More than likely this New York City lady didn't think of him at all, he told himself. And if she did, it was to wonder if he was capable of solving this murder and getting Rowdy back, but not in that order.

"What's got you over there scowling like that?" he asked.

"My father was murdered."

He shook his head. "We both know that's not it." For a few moments he thought she was going to take offense.

"Georgia told me that I'm the beneficiary of a million-dollar insurance policy on Rowdy."

"You hadn't known?"

"How could I?" she demanded. "I haven't seen or talked to my father in years. I know Georgia's worried that she'll lose her job if her company has to pay out, but…"

"But?"

"She all but accused me of working with my father to rip off the insurance company by having him murdered and Rowdy stolen."

He'd considered that the moment he'd heard about the million-dollar policy. People plotted murder for a lot less money than that. "You're saying you didn't?"

"No," she snapped indignantly. "Why would I come here demanding you find Rowdy if I didn't want him to be found?"

"For show, to make yourself look innocent because you knew the dummy would never be found? Or to make sure that it isn't found." He saw her angry expression. "Just spitballing here. You did ask."

She sat back, crossing her arms over her ample chest and sighing angrily.

Ahead, he concentrated on the turnoff into the ranch and slowed. He knew of the Crandell family. He might have met the old man years ago at a rodeo in Eureka. What he did know about them was that they stayed to themselves. He'd heard there'd been some kind of accident, a death involving one of the sons. Didn't seem like that was why they'd isolated themselves from the community at large, but he supposed it was possible. Out here, the ranches were so far apart, it was easy to keep to yourself if it was what you wanted.

Bringing Molly along had been impulsive and yet he'd hoped she might open up to him on the drive. There was also the chance that she might see something out here at the ranch that would jar a memory about her father. Right now, he'd take any help he could get solving this murder.

As he drove into the ranch yard though, he worried about the kind of reception he might get. Even though he was in his uniform, driving a patrol SUV with the sheriff's department logo on the side, it wouldn't be the first time he'd found himself facing angry armed men.

This time he realized wasn't going to be any different as he saw a man come out of the first house carrying a shotgun.

MOLLY HAD ALREADY decided that this was a mistake even before she spotted the angry-looking elderly man with the shotgun. The sheriff had made it sound as if they were just going for a ride, but he was much cagier than she'd realized. He had an ulterior motive in bringing her along. He wanted to question her about the million-dollar payout if Rowdy wasn't found.

Just because he was sheriff and lived in a small town in the middle of nowhere didn't mean he wasn't sharp and knew what he was doing. She hoped that was true as she considered the man with the shotgun.

"Stay in the car," the sheriff said as he parked and climbed out. He didn't have to tell her twice as she watched the man standing on the porch shift his shotgun.

"Afternoon," she heard the sheriff say congenially.

"You're trespassing," the man said in a deep scratchy voice. He looked to be close to ninety or older, a big man who'd once been bigger, but still appeared in decent shape for his age. "Unless you have a warrant—"

"Not that kind of visit," the sheriff said. "Just need to know if any of you have heard of a man named Clay Wheaton." No response.

Molly could see that this wasn't going to get them anywhere, just as she'd thought. She looked around the ranch seeing a couple of old barns, some smaller houses, a few outbuildings, farm machinery and a large tree next to a creek.

Her pulse jumped at the sight of the black tire tied to a rope hanging from one of the largest of the tree's limbs. The tree was huge, looked old. Even from where she sat in the patrol SUV, she could see the scarred trunk. It almost looked as if there were names carved into the trunk's base.

She opened her door, feeling like a sleepwalker, as she got out and walked toward the tree. She heard voices behind her, including the sheriff's trying to call her back, but she kept going. She had to see what was carved into that tree.

Even as she kept walking, the logical part of her brain was arguing that she wouldn't find her father's name carved there. That it was only a made-up story, one of many stories Rowdy told about growing up on a ranch. The sheriff and his theories about Rowdy's brand were just that. Fiction. She'd be lucky if the old man didn't shoot her in the back. It would be all the sheriff's fault since he was the one who'd brought her out here, she told herself.

A few feet from the swing, she stopped. There were names carved in the tree's trunk—just like she'd thought. Seth, Jo, Pat, Gage, Cliff, Wyatt, Ty—there were more but the one name she'd expected to see hadn't been there. No Clay. Someone grabbed her arm, dragged her back from the tree.

"Are you trying to get us both killed?" the

sheriff whispered hoarsely. "We need to leave." She heard the urgency in his voice and yet she found herself trying to pull away. Clay had to be there. She'd heard the story about this tree and the names. She'd been so convinced that she would find it… "We need to leave. *Now*."

With a jolt, she realized how foolish she'd been. Clay wasn't there because he'd made the story up for Rowdy to tell. It wasn't even an original story, a tire swing, a big old tree, a pocketknife and a lazy warm summer day, plenty of time to carve a name in a tree. Probably every kid who didn't live in an apartment in the city had done the same thing.

She let the sheriff pull her back from the tree. As she turned, she saw that there were more men now standing in front of the other houses, all armed, all looking angry. "Sorry," she called to them. Their responses were steely glares.

As she tried to swallow, her mouth gone dry, she couldn't believe how foolish she'd been. The sheriff was right, she could get them killed and for what? Some story she'd once heard out of the mouth of a dummy?

The sheriff opened her car door and practically shoved her inside. She didn't hear what he said, but he seemed to get behind the wheel quick enough. As they were driving away, she saw him glancing back until they reached the county road and were off the Crandell Ranch.

"What the hell was that about back there?" he demanded.

She was embarrassed to tell him, especially after she'd told him that nothing about Clay Wheaton was real. Or that she hadn't seen her father's shows or cared about him or what he'd left her. Yet, she'd bought into it the moment she'd seen that tree and the tire swing next to the creek. It was exactly as he had described it. Rowdy had described it, she reminded herself with a sigh. "You were so convinced that Rowdy's brand meant something..."

"I was wrong, but that still doesn't explain what you were doing getting out of the car when I told you not to. Those men with guns were serious. You could have been shot. Going on someone's property without permission—or a warrant—is serious business in this state. Well?"

Molly could hear in his voice that he wasn't going to quit asking until she told him, as embarrassing as it was. "When I saw that tire swing and that big tree, I remembered this story Rowdy used to tell as part of his act. I don't even recall the punch line, just that as a boy he'd carved his name into a big ol' tree with a tire swing hanging from it out on the ranch." She looked over at the sheriff, surprised he hadn't said anything.

"Was his name there?"

She shook her head. "It was just a silly made-up story like all of them that he told." She looked away. "I can't believe I bought into it. But if the brand really meant something..."

Molly expected him to call her on blaming him for the foolish thing she'd just done. Instead, he drove in silence for a few minutes before he looked over at her and asked, "When did you go see his show?"

She realized her mistake. She'd told him that her father had performed for her and her mother, that he'd been terrible, that he'd left them. She'd made it sound as if she'd never seen him again.

A lump formed in her throat. She hated being caught in a lie. She swallowed before she answered, feeling that almost getting them both killed he deserved honesty, for once. "In college. I went with some friends who wanted to go." She shrugged. "I didn't talk to him." But he had seen her. Their eyes had met. He'd sent a note that he wanted to see her. She'd balled it up, tossed it in the trash on the way out of the auditorium.

The sheriff was quiet again for several miles. "I'm sorry the trip was a wild goose chase. The men I spoke with swore they'd never heard of Clay Wheaton. How about something to eat in the big city of Eureka before the café closes?"

BRANDT'S EMOTIONS VEERED back and forth from furious with Molly to feeling sorry for her. When her stomach growled in answer to his question, he felt a kinship since he was starved. "When was the last time you ate?"

She had to think apparently. "Yesterday, on the plane?"

"Well, we need to remedy that and fast since Trappers Saloon closes at eight."

"Eight in the evening?" She said it as if she couldn't imagine eating before nine.

"It's still off season here. You're not in New York anymore," he said with a laugh.

"Tell me about it," she added, looking out the window. It was already dark as he drove into Eureka. "I always wondered why my father chose the cowboy outfit for him and Rowdy. All of it seemed so fake, the cowboy hero, so big, so strong, so capable. Yet since I arrived here, all I see are cowboy hats, boots and trucks."

He laughed. "It's real—it's just not as glamorous as some people try to make it out to be. For many in this state, it's a way of life, a dying one for some since ranching isn't always profitable."

"What keeps Fortune Creek alive?" she asked once they were seated inside the Trappers Saloon. They'd called it close. The place would be closing for the day soon. For that reason it was almost empty already.

He watched her studying the menu. "It's home for a lot of us. Some, like Ash, came back after a successful career and invested in the town. Me, it's home, way up here in the northwest corner of the state near the boundary line with Idaho and Canada. See something you like?"

She glanced up and grinned before diving back into the menu. "Montana sushi? Thin-sliced sirloin, served medium rare or rare only, on a bed of lettuce with sweet chili huckleberry sauce." She looked up at him again. "Huckleberries?"

"They're delicious, picked around here in the summer. You should try them. Might want to try the Wild Thing elk burger."

"Elk? I think I'll stick with chicken. It is really chicken, right?"

He grinned. "It's not sage hen, I promise."

"Sage hen?"

"Sorry, local joke." He ordered the Hang Over burger with huckleberry slaw and she went with the Pacific salmon served with couscous & veggies. "Don't feel like living dangerously, huh?" She shook her head. "Tell me about yourself. What does a financial analyst do?"

"I'm sure you'd find it boring—most people do." He waited and she finally said, "I work for a stock brokerage. I examine financial information in order to help clients looking for businesses to invest in."

"No kidding."

She smiled and this one reached her eyes. "Told you it was boring."

"It must not be for you."

"It's not. It's something solid. Numbers don't lie."

He was no psychologist, but he couldn't help but wonder if the job hadn't attracted her because of what her father had done for a living.

Their food came. She picked at hers. He offered her a bite of his hamburger, then his huckleberry slaw.

"This is delicious."

He motioned to the waitress to bring them another burger and slaw and take away the salmon. They split both meals. After that she seemed to relax as the restaurant closed and they left in a companionable silence.

"You must think I'm heartless," she said as they headed back to Fortune Creek. "I'm sorry my father was murdered. I'm just so angry with him."

"I get it. Parents often disappoint us, some worse than others."

"Not many take off to be ventriloquists."

"No, that's true enough." He felt her gaze on him.

"I just don't understand why the killer took Rowdy," she said.

He shook his head. "Professional jealousy?"

"Not hardly. I don't think my father's been performing for quite a few years now. At one time, he had a show in Vegas and was doing well. Then he just disappeared."

So she *had* kept track of him more than she'd

admitted, he thought. "Would you really chop up Rowdy?"

"I don't know." She turned to look out the window. "Pretty petty being jealous of a dummy, huh."

"My dad had a dog that he loved more than me and that dog used to bite him all the time for no reason." He felt her gaze again. "I'm serious." That bow-shaped mouth turned up a little at the corners, her gaze saying she wasn't sure what to believe about his story—let alone him.

She was quiet most of the ride back. He left her with her thoughts, enjoying the drive and the company. She kept surprising him. He was glad that his first impression of her had been wrong.

"Thank you for tonight," she said as the lights of Fortune Creek appeared high on the side of the mountain. "I loved that restaurant. Next time I want to try the elk burger."

He smiled. Next time? That made it sound as if she was planning to hang around for a while. "You'll have to try Alice Weatherbee's huckleberry pie at the Fortune Creek Cafe. It's the best. You haven't tried it yet, have you?"

She shook her head.

He'd been fishing, wondering about the takeout container he'd found in her father's pickup. He was still waiting for possible fingerprints and DNA. Still wondering who her father had given a ride to.

Molly hadn't flown to Montana earlier than she'd said, but she could have driven and stayed out of sight. Against his better judgment, he was hoping like hell that she had nothing to do with murder—let alone deception.

Chapter Seven

The next morning while having a mug of coffee in his office, the sheriff looked up to see a pickup with a camper on the back pull in. Arkansas plates? That was a new one in Fortune Creek, he thought.

A young woman stepped out. Her black hair hung in a long braid. She wore an ankle-length flowered dress and what looked like combat boots as if she'd been dropped from the 1960s. The camper, he saw, was covered in activist stickers with a smattering of political ones too.

"Oh boy," Brandt said, just imaging how some of the conservative older cowboys were going to react. Helen was already staring out the window, her mouth gaping open, as the young woman headed for the front door.

"I'll handle this one," he said, stepping out of his small office to greet the newcomer. "I'm Sheriff Brandt Parker. Can I help you?"

She grinned, cocking her head to the side. "Howdy,

Sheriff. You're just the person I want to see. I'm here about Clay Wheaton."

That took him by surprise, but only for a second as he wondered how many more people would show up. He couldn't wait to hear why this woman was interested in the ventriloquist. Or, like the other two women, was she here about Rowdy the dummy? "Why don't you step into my office?"

"Mind if I bring in my dog first?" She turned to Helen. "You wouldn't have a small dish of water, would you?"

"No," Helen said, but the woman either didn't hear or ignored her as she went back out to her truck and opened the passenger-side door. He couldn't see because of the sun glinting off the windshield, but he was expecting something large. He was amused when she brought in a tiny white ball of fur.

"Her name's Ghost," she said as she handed the dog to Helen, who, startled, took it automatically even though she was no fan of dogs. "Just a little water would be great." With that the women headed for Brandt's office.

Offering her a chair, the sheriff walked around his desk to sit down. He could see Helen still standing in the middle of the outer office staring at the fur ball in her hands. "What can I do for you, Ms....?"

"Jessica Woods." She turned to look out the

window at the hotel across the street. "That's where Clay was murdered?"

"Did you know him?"

She turned back around. "No, I heard about it when I was doing some investigating on another case next door in Idaho. I figured I'd better come up and check it out."

Investigating? Case? "Are you…" He was thinking undercover DEA.

"I'm a paranormal investigator." At his no doubt confused look, she added, "I have a PhD in parapsychology science with a masters in folklore. I'm here to investigate claims that Clay Wheaton's vent figure sang for a half hour after the puppeteer died. I would like to examine Rowdy the Rodeo Cowboy."

He nodded and leaned back in his chair as he searched for words. "I'm afraid you won't be able examine Mr. Wheaton's dummy. At this point, we suspect the killer may have taken it with him."

"Seriously? You don't have it?" She sounded devastated.

"No." He didn't mention that she wasn't the only one interested in Rowdy.

"That is so disappointing," she said. "But once you find the killer, you'll retrieve the dummy." She got to her feet as if the problem was solved. Her gaze went to the hotel across the street. "I guess Ghost and I will go check out the hotel then. I've heard this isn't the first paranormal event that has happened there. Let me know when you find Rowdy. I'll be staying in my camper down by the creek," she said as she left his office.

He watched her retrieve Ghost from Helen. To his amazement, Helen seemed taken with the dog and appeared reluctant to return it.

His cell phone rang. "Sheriff Parker," he said distractedly as he watched Helen say goodbye to Ghost as if the dog had become a long-lost friend.

"Thought you'd want to know."

He realized that he'd missed what the coroner had said. "Sorry, JP, what's that?"

"Got a hit on your victim's DNA. It came back a lot sooner than expected because he was in the military. That's not all. Are you sitting down?"

MOLLY HADN'T SLEPT WELL. Even the hot shower this morning hadn't helped. At one point she'd awakened from a dream, but as she sat up, she would have sworn that she had heard the last few refrains of Rowdy singing one of his cowboy songs.

Her heart had pounded in her ears as goosebumps raced across her skin. It had sounded so real. No wonder she'd had trouble getting back to sleep last night.

She was thinking about going back to bed when she got the call from the sheriff.

"Could you stop by my office?" He'd sounded so officious, so different from last night at the café in Eureka that whatever he wanted must be serious. She quickly dressed and headed for his office.

Last night after she'd returned from her trip with the sheriff, she'd gone for a walk. Only the bar had still been open. The convenience-grocery was closing. She'd stopped to visit with the older woman who ran the place. She'd glanced into the front windows of a narrow building after seeing a post office sign in the window. It had the smallest post office she'd ever seen along the right side at the front of the store.

"You the one from New York City?" the elderly woman had inquired pleasantly enough.

"I am," she'd admitted, amused by the way the woman had said it. "Have you ever been there?"

That got a crackle out of her. "Don't need gas, do you?" She'd told her that she didn't. "Good, cuz, I turn off the gas pumps at night." The pumps looked old, from another era. "You can come at six in the morning though, fill up and then come inside to tell me how many gallons you got and pay for your gas before you leave town."

"I'll keep that in mind, thanks. But I'm not leaving town for a while."

"Well, in that case." The woman had wiped her hand on her canvas pants and held it out. "Name's Cora. Cora Green."

"Molly Lockhart."

Cora had frowned. "Lockhart. I thought your name would be Wheaton." She had chin-length gray hair, green eyes and a fading beauty. Molly guessed that she'd given cowboys around here a run for their money when she was younger. Heck, she probably still did. "You're not married, divorced?"

"No, I just changed my name. It's a long story."

"All the sad ones are, aren't they? You have a nice night." With that Cora went back inside the store-gas station and finished locking up behind her.

As the woman turned off the pumps and the lights, Molly had walked to the end of town, which wasn't far. It ended abruptly at a creek. She'd thought of the people who called Fortune Creek home, including the sheriff. She'd never met anyone who lived in a town a block long that dead-ended at a creek. There was only one way out of Fortune Creek—the way you came in.

This place was so different from New York City. Not just Fortune Creek, which wasn't much of a town at all, but the people. To say it was a simpler lifestyle was almost humorous.

As she'd reached the creek, she'd spotted a pickup and camper parked at the water's edge. She could hear the faint crackle of a campfire, smell the smoke and feel a chill as if suddenly aware of how the temperature had dropped.

She'd turned back, leaving the ambient light of the campfire to walk through the darkness of what felt like a ghost town. Suddenly, she was anxious to get back to the hotel as she recalled there was a killer out there somewhere.

Earlier she'd been glad that she hadn't run into Georgia after their argument—but on her walk to the hotel she'd been sorry she had no one to talk to about any of this. What friends she had would already be in bed back East. There was no man in her life, after parting ways months ago. She'd never felt more alone.

"Enjoy your walk?" the hotel owner had asked as she came in through the lobby.

"I did." She'd stopped, curious. "So have you lived here your whole life?"

Ash Hammond had nodded as if not the first time he'd been asked this. "I left for college, the NFL, but yes, I came back and bought the hotel and have been renovating it. And before you ask, no, I'm not expecting a lot of guests."

She had laughed as well since it was as if he'd read her mind. "Sorry, it is just in such an out-of-the-way place."

"We get tourists in the summer—some people get lost and end up here for the night," he'd admitted with a chuckle. "With the latest publicity, more will be coming, thanks to your father."

She'd frowned. "Him dying in your hotel?"

He'd shaken his head. "No, sorry, the dummy. The older couple who was in the nearby room swore they heard Rowdy singing after...you know."

"That's not possible. You do know the dummy doesn't talk without the ventriloquist, right? So with Clay dead, Rowdy wasn't singing."

Ash had shrugged. "Just telling you what they said they heard. Since they went to the press with the story, it will probably be like last time."

"What happened last time?"

"Rumors of the hotel being haunted brought ghost hunters out of the woodwork," he'd said and smiled. "I can see that you're a skeptic. Me too. I've had this place for over a year. Haven't seen a ghost yet."

"That's…comforting," she'd said. "Though it is interesting what the older couple in the next room said they'd heard. It could mean that the killer was still in the room manipulating the dummy."

He'd frowned. "Wouldn't the killer also have to be an impersonator? Seems unlikely."

"As unlikely as a dummy coming to life and singing because his master was dead?"

"You have a point," he'd said with another chuckle. He had a great smile and was handsome, if you liked that big brawny good-looking type. She preferred a leaner solid look. Like the sheriff. The thought had made her realize just how tired she was.

She'd said good night and gone up to bed, before falling dead asleep. But her slumber was haunted by weird dreams that left her feeling uneasy even in the light of day.

MOLLY SMELLED LIKE SUNSHINE, the sheriff thought as he led her into his office and closed the door. Her hair, long and blond, was tucked up into a rather messy ball at the nape of her slim neck. He thought that was the style nowadays. But he also thought she might have hurried after her morning shower because her hair appeared to still be damp. He feared he'd awakened her, which only made him wonder when she'd gotten to bed last night. From his upstairs apartment, he'd seen her wandering down the street toward the bar last night.

"Please have a seat," he said as he took his chair behind the desk. He couldn't help thinking about everything Coroner JP Brown had told him. There'd been so much off about this case right from the get-go.

"Peculiar case," the coroner had said earlier on the phone, once he knew he had the sheriff's attention. "Like the ink." JP had cleared his voice. "It was all over the fingers of the deceased's right hand."

"And this is important how?" Brandt had to ask.

"He was writing something with a leaky pen before he died."

The sheriff had chuckled. "He left a note on the hotel stationery with two names and phone numbers to be called in an emergency it said. There were ink drops on it and a smudge."

"*Before* he was murdered? As if he knew he was about to die?"

"Maybe. Maybe it was something the man did on a regular basis, traveling alone and being of an age." He remembered something that hadn't struck him as terribly odd before. "Neither the leaky pen nor any of the hotel stationery that Ash supplies to the rooms was found."

"Can't imagine why the killer would have taken a leaky pen, let alone the stationery," JP said. "Maybe simply because it was free."

"I guess, but why would the killer leave the note Clay had written? Because the killer had wanted the next of kin notified? Or because it didn't matter?"

"Interesting," the coroner had said. "Didn't you tell me that the man's daughter is in town?"

JP's question had rattled him. If there was even a chance that the killer had wanted her to come to Fortune Creek, then Molly Lockhart could be in danger.

"Anyway, you're probably more interested in the DNA," the coroner had said and dropped the real bombshell.

As Molly took a chair across from him, Brandt met her gaze. This morning her eyes were like a tropical sea of blues and greens. "You were right about your father." Hadn't she told him that she thought Clay was a phony? She raised a brow. "Clay Wheaton wasn't his real name. When his DNA was run, it brought up his military service record. Did you know your father was in the military?" From her expression she hadn't. "He enlisted at seventeen with the name he was born with, Seth Crandell. According to the information he provided at that time, he was the son of Irma and Cecil Crandell with a rural address outside of Eureka, Montana."

"*Crandell?* From the ranch where we went yesterday?"

He nodded. "I believe that elderly man who came out with the shotgun is Cecil, his father. Did you see the name Seth carved in the tree?"

Her eyes widened. "*Seth.* I saw the name carved into the tree trunk." He could see her putting the pieces together. "The story he told through Rowdy about the pocketknife and the tree hadn't been something he made up."

She hugged herself as if feeling a chill. "If that's the case then…then maybe the other stories were true too." She looked at him with a kind of wonder. She had a heart-shaped face with bow lips, her skin porcelain smooth. In the shaft of sunlight pouring into his office from the front windows he wondered how he hadn't noticed before how beautiful she was.

He blinked, realizing that she'd asked him a question. "Sorry?"

"Couldn't that explain what he was doing here if those people are his family?"

His thought exactly. "Your family too." He saw that she hadn't made that leap yet. "And there's more." She seemed to brace herself, looking expectantly at him, but also wary. "I'm sorry, but your father had cancer at a stage where if he hadn't been murdered, he would have had only weeks to live."

MOLLY TOOK THE news like a blow. Now she knew what her father had been doing here in Fortune Creek. "He'd come here to see his family before he died."

The realization came with the familiar bitter taste. Her father had come here to see his *other* family—not *her*. He'd come to see the Crandells, those odd people she'd seen yesterday.

It was as if the sheriff was thinking the same thing. "He might have had some loose ends to tie up here before he…"

She shook her head. "Before he came to tell me goodbye?" She was on her feet, angry with herself for coming here. All of this was too much to take in. She'd told herself she was doing this because she needed closure and destroying Rowdy would give it to her. The more she learned about her father, the more she didn't want to be here, the more she didn't care what had happened to him or his dummy.

"For whatever reason, he'd changed his name and became a ventriloquist," the sheriff said. "Maybe there is something about him he needed to hide behind Rowdy—and hide from you."

"His whole life was a lie even if his silly cowboy stories were true," she said. "So what if he was running from something? Hiding behind the dummy? Whatever it was, he'd come back here to..." She looked at him as if she expected him to fill in the blanks and remembered what Georgia had told her. "He'd been here before."

"Maybe," the sheriff said. "He asked for room 401 next to the fire escape, but given what we now know..."

"Someone could have told him to take that room," she said with a start.

"Maybe. There's a chance he'd been expecting company. We suspect the killer used the fire escape to enter and exit the hotel. There's no alarm on that door, but when closed, it's locked. That night someone had propped the door open with a book. Your father wrote the note with your name and phone number on it, along with his insurance agent's."

"He knew he was going to be killed. So basically, he was committing suicide by murder?"

The sheriff shook his head. "You realize this is all conjecture. We have no proof."

"He changed his name. Doesn't that sound like he had something to hide? Something to fear by staying Seth Crandell? If so, then he had to have known returning here would be dangerous. You don't think one of the Crandells killed him? His own family?"

"Not necessarily. But they might know who would want to harm him."

She groaned. "How could I not know this?" she demanded of herself more than the sheriff. "The clues were all there. That ridiculous brand on Rowdy's case. I never dreamed it was any more real than his cowboy costume or my father's."

A few moments ago, she'd wanted to walk away from all of this, regretting coming here. Now though, she knew she couldn't leave without finding out the truth. She said as much to the sheriff and saw his expression change.

"I'm not sure that's a good idea." He seemed to hesitate before he continued. "The killer took the pen your father used to leave your phone number and the extra hotel stationery. But the killer left behind the note with your name and number and Georgia Eden's." She waited, not sure what he was getting at. "The killer might have wanted you to come to Fortune Creek."

Molly frowned. "Why?"

"That's what I don't know. But you could be in danger."

She stared at him for a moment before shaking her head. "I'm not leaving until I know who killed my father—and why. I guess that means I'm going to have to go back out to the Crandell Ranch."

"Whoa!" He held up his hands, no doubt hearing the determination in her voice. "Way too dangerous. For all we know one of them killed your father."

"You're planning to go back out there, aren't you?"

"On official business this time."

She met his gaze. "Take me with you."

"Bad idea."

"Then I'll go alone."

"That is an even worse idea. Maybe you didn't pick up on the tension out there the other day. You could be shot as a trespasser. In Montana, that is definitely not unheard of."

"If you're trying to tell me that things are different here, I've already figured that out." She gave him an impatient look. "If they have the answers, then I need to talk to them. Seth was their son. That makes me their granddaughter."

"If they killed one of their own, I doubt you being Seth's daughter will hold much sway with them," he said, trying to reason with her.

She dug in, seeing that it didn't really surprise him. "I'm going, one way or the other."

He swore under his breath. "Promise me you won't go alone…" He rushed on before she could speak. "And I'll let you ride along with me. But you have to do what I tell you. The Crandells could be dangerous."

"I have to know why my father changed his name, why he left here, why he came back and why he kept it all a secret to his death," she said. "Those people back at that ranch know."

"I suspect they might," he said, though sounding reluctant. "But that doesn't mean that they're going to tell me. Keep in mind, we're dealing with possible murderers."

"And kidnappers. Let's not forget Rowdy."

"Yes," he said with a groan. "Let's not forget Rowdy."

Chapter Eight

With time to kill before the sheriff could make the trip out to the Crandell Ranch again, he suggested Molly get some breakfast. "You wouldn't leave without me," she said, stopping in his office doorway to look back at him.

"No," he said, not appearing happy about it. "I wouldn't dream of it."

She nodded and left to walk down to the Fortune Creek Café. Along the way she passed several empty lots and the empty stone building that she'd noticed last night. The structure appeared to have been a bank. It was small with large windows across the front.

There was something about it that drew her closer. She stopped to peer in the windows. Inside, she was delighted to see an old tin ceiling, hardwood floors and oak cabinets that ran from floor to ceiling on one side. It appeared that after the bank closed, the building had been used as some kind of shop.

She could imagine it as a place that sold unique

handcrafted one-of-kind items. People would drive all the way to Fortune Creek just to buy them. Maybe. If not, there was always an online business using photographs of a shop for promo. She decided she would mention it to a couple of the investors who might be interested. She'd work up a cost analysis when she returned, she thought with excitement. She'd ask the sheriff who owned the building and how much they might want for it.

Molly stopped herself. She needed to get breakfast so she'd be ready to leave when the sheriff was. But she couldn't get the building and the potential shop out of her mind since once she'd seen it, she could now imagine it as if it was already a done deal.

On down the street, she pushed open the café door to the smell of fried bacon and coffee. Her stomach rumbled as she started to step in and saw Georgia. She was sitting with a young woman with coal-black hair that had been plaited into one long braid. The two sat at a small table by the window.

She put her head down, pretending not to have seen them, and started for another table at the back.

"Molly," Georgia called to her. "Come join us. There's someone you need to meet."

She turned, pretending surprise to see the two of them sitting there, and headed for the table all smiles as if she and Georgia hadn't argued yesterday.

Georgia did the introductions as Molly took the free chair. "This is Jessica Woods. She's camped down by the creek."

Molly had seen the camp last night. But she couldn't imagine why Georgia thought she'd need to meet this woman with her hippie clothing and a little white furball of a dog in a basket beside her chair.

"And this is Ghost," Jessica said motioning to the dog. "She helps me with my research."

"Research?" Molly repeated.

"I'm a parapsychologist," Jessica said and smiled. "A ghost hunter and Ghost helps me."

"Guess why she's in Fortune Creek," Georgia said, then blurted out, "She's here about Rowdy the Rodeo Cowboy."

Molly stared at Georgia, then at the woman. Jessica was younger than both she and Georgia but not by much. "What do you want with Rowdy?"

"The singing," Georgia said. "She wants to find out if Clay reached out to Rowdy from the other side or if Rowdy has always been the conduit for paranormal occurrences."

She stared at one woman, then the other, speechless. *She'd thought she'd heard Rowdy singing last night.* The memory came back so sharp and crisp that she would have sworn it had been real. But her father was dead so common sense told her that story was just part of this ongoing nightmare.

"I really doubt—" But Georgia cut her off, asking about the woman's dog's abilities. Fortunately, a plump brown-haired woman came out of the kitchen with a full pot of coffee. She filled a cup for Molly and took her order. "I'd like an egg white omelet with—"

"She'll take bacon and those delicious pancakes, you make, Alice."

As the woman refilled Georgia's coffee cup, she smiled. "You sure you don't want another pancake or two, Georgia? You could use some meat on those bones."

Georgia laughed and said, "The pancakes were delicious, but I'm full as a tick." The woman's laugh followed her all the way to the kitchen.

Jessica excused herself to leave for an appointment with Ash Hammond, the owner of the hotel. She scooped up the basket with the dog and left.

"What was all that about?" Molly demanded, slightly annoyed that wherever Georgia went she seemed to make friends. It wasn't a talent Molly had herself. "Ghost hunter? Pancakes and bacon?"

"You'll love the cakes," Georgia said dismissing her complaint. "It's also the special today so that's really all Alice is set up to make. That's why there aren't menus." She waved all that away and leaned conspiratorially across the table. "Do you believe this? Jessica is looking for Rowdy too. Who else is going to show up wanting the dummy?"

"That's the part you're having trouble believing?" Molly asked and then laughed, Georgia joining her. She marveled at this woman. She seemed at home no matter where it was. Even here in this strange little town.

"Maybe there's something to it," Georgia was saying. "Otherwise, how do you explain the dummy singing after your father was dead?"

She shook her head. That was just it; she couldn't explain any of this. Having just learned that Clay Wheaton was really Seth Crandell, the son of Cecil who'd almost shot her yesterday, she felt off-balance. That was enough to try to get her head around without attempting to understand why the elderly couple thought they'd heard Rowdy singing after her father had died. Clearly, they had been mistaken about the time.

"How'd your trip go with the sheriff yesterday?" Georgia asked as Alice brought out her breakfast and refilled their coffee cups, commenting on the beautiful day and complimenting the blouse Georgia was wearing.

Molly waited until Alice had gone back to the kitchen. Yesterday during their argument, she and Georgia had felt like adversaries. Which she now thought was silly. They both wanted the same thing. Kind of. Also, could she really blame Georgia for being suspicious of her given the million-dollar insurance policy?

But mostly she needed someone to confide in since who knew how long they would be here. She needed Georgia's down-home take on this mess.

"Turns out Clay Wheaton wasn't his real name."

The woman's eyes widened. "What do you mean?"

"Apparently, he'd changed it after he got out of the military before he'd met my mother. It looks like he might be related to a ranch family from around here."

"Well, that would explain what he was doing here," Georgia agreed. "Bad blood between him and the family, you think?"

"Looks that way since someone killed him and who else did he know around here?"

"Good question. I was looking on a map. The closest town of any size is Eureka."

"We went there last night. I highly recommend the Trappers Saloon, anything with huckleberries."

There was a twinkle in Georgia's eye. "You and the sheriff?"

"It wasn't like that." She felt a flush start at her throat and rise to her cheeks.

"Right. He's drop-dead gorgeous, or are you going to tell me you didn't notice?"

She'd noticed a lot about him. She'd felt his strength as he'd gripped her arm yesterday, seen his kindness and generosity when he'd shared his meal and ordered another and witnessed his fear for her when she'd defied him and gotten out of the patrol SUV at the Crandell Ranch.

She quickly changed the subject. "You're welcome to take the rental car if you want to go into Eureka. The sheriff and I are going back out to the ranch to see if anyone will admit to my father being a relative. Oh, and Clay was dying. He didn't have long at all to live."

Georgia was shaking her head. "I never would have guessed he had secrets. He seemed…sad."

Sad. Molly tried not to think about that, still angry with him for abandoning her without any explanation. "The sheriff mentioned that maybe someone my father knew had told him to ask for room 401 because it is right by the fire escape stairs. He could have even left the door propped open for his killer."

"As if he knew one of them would be coming for him."

"It's made me realize how little I know about my father," she said truthfully. "He left when I was nine. Not even my mother seemed to know much about his early years. I wish I could ask her, but she passed almost ten years ago now. There's no one to ask. Except the Crandells. And they might not be inclined to tell me anything."

"I'm sorry. All of this must come as a shock." Georgia seemed lost in thought for a moment.

"It occurs to me that if you're right and Clay was from around here, a lot of people other than his family must have known him. You said he went into the military under his real name, right?"

"Enlisted at seventeen."

"So, his parents had to sign for him," Georgia said. "That's telling. But if he lived here seventeen years, then he must have gone to school, right? He must have had friends."

Molly nodded. "The answer does seem to be here. I'm staying around for a while to see what I can find out."

"I'm not leaving until I find Rowdy," Georgia said with a groan. "I might have to spend the rest of my life in Fortune Creek."

"Once the sheriff finds the killer…" Not even Molly held out much hope.

"I'm just worried that the killer could have already tried to sell Rowdy," Georgia was saying. "I've been watching for him online. I was thinking about offering a reward."

Molly hadn't thought that the killer had taken the dummy thinking it was worth money on the open market. For some reason, she'd thought it was more personal, like her own desire to get her hands on Rowdy. "Seems foolish to try to sell it if you were the murderer."

"Murder is pretty foolish when you think about it."

She couldn't argue that as she dug into her breakfast. Georgia was right. The pancakes were delish and so was the bacon. She couldn't help thinking that if the murderer was that clueless, then why not offer a reward and catch him?

"I think a reward is a good idea." They decided on a thousand dollars, Georgia saying she'd pay most of it since she had the most to lose but Molly insisted that they split it. "Okay, I'll get right on it."

Molly ate as if famished. She blamed all this fresh air up here in the wilds of Montana. When Alice came back to refill her coffee, Molly asked if Clay Wheaton had eaten his meals here.

"The man with the doll?" The woman belly laughed. "That was a first. Saw him talking to it like it was alive. I just figured he wasn't in his right mind. He seemed harmless enough."

Molly felt a wave of sadness for her father, realizing how lonely his life must have been. Had he come back here to die? To mend fences? Surely not to be murdered. But apparently, he'd known that it could happen—and it did. She thought of Rowdy and all those years he and her father were inseparable. Of course, the dummy didn't sing after her father was killed.

But if Rowdy could have, she realized he would have—just as the couple said, and that gave her a chill.

Chapter Nine

When Molly returned to the hotel, she spotted Georgia in what appeared to be serious conversation with Jessica, the younger woman she'd met that morning. She had a sudden strange uncharitable thought. What if the two were making some kind of deal? If one of them found Rowdy first—

"Molly." Georgia motioned her over to the corner where the two had been so intensely engaged. "Jessica wants in."

Still caught up in her thought of a behind-her-back deal, she said, "Wants in on what?"

"The reward," Jessica said. "I'll match whatever the two of you suggest."

"You will?" She couldn't help her surprise. Why had she gotten the feeling that Jessica might have to borrow money for gas to leave Fortune Creek? Because she hadn't had breakfast or even a cup of coffee at the café earlier? Or because she was staying in her camper down by the river? "Sure."

They decided to keep the reward at a thousand and not go any higher for the time being. Jessica took her dog and started to leave, stopping to talk to Ash for a moment. From what Molly could tell, the two were at odds. Ash was shaking his head and not looking the least bit happy as she left.

"You're sure about this?" she asked Georgia, who shrugged.

"I thought we should at least ask her if she was interested. She wants Rowdy as much as we do. I already told Cora Green at that little store about the reward." Georgia grinned. "As talkative as she is, I figure she'll let people around here know. I'm also putting it in the Eureka both print and online newspaper, *Tobacco Valley News*, and the local shopper."

"Sounds good," Molly said distractedly. She couldn't get Jessica off her mind. "What's with her and Ash?"

"She wants to investigate the hotel for paranormal activity while she's waiting for Rowdy to be found. Apparently, Ash isn't wild about the idea. She plans to get a room and do the investigating on her own. She seems very determined."

As the front door opened, Molly caught a glint in Georgia's eye as Deputy Jaden Montgomery strode in. He stopped in the middle of the lobby, pushing back his Stetson as he called out a hello to Ash.

"I'm going to do some investigating of my own with a little help from that handsome deputy," Georgia said with a grin. "Wish me luck." And with that, she was off, calling, "Deputy, a moment of your time."

As Molly started for the elevator, her cell phone rang. It was the sheriff.

BRANDT REALIZED THERE was no way he would have been able to keep a lid on the murder—even if the story about the singing ventriloquist's dummy hadn't gone viral. It wasn't every day that a ventriloquist was killed in Fortune Creek, Montana—let alone his dummy missing.

He was just getting ready to leave after his call to Molly when Helen came in with her "more-bad-news face." He groaned. "Now what?"

"A thousand-dollar reward is being offered for the dummy."

"Molly?" Helen nodded and waited. *"Georgia?"* Another nod and still she stood, hip cocked, in his office doorway. "If you tell me Jessica Woods—" She nodded and left, closing the door behind her so he could swear in peace.

"Jessica Woods?" he repeated to himself. She had a stake in finding Rowdy, but she didn't appear to be someone who had money to throw away.

He wished that they had asked him about offering a reward for Rowdy. Now the killer knew the dummy was worth something. Maybe worse, the killer might also realize that the dummy could be worth even more. He shook his head, reminded of who he was dealing with—three very determined young women.

As Molly came through the front door of the sheriff's department, he tamped down his anger and frustration. He could understand Georgia's desperation in finding Rowdy. He could even see Jessica wanting to get her hands on the dummy, but Molly? Was she really willing to pay good money to get Rowdy back so she could destroy it? Also, if found, she was out a million dollars.

That thought made him uneasy. Maybe she had her reasons for playing along pretending to look for Rowdy, offering a reward, saying she just wanted to put an end to the doll. Or maybe she and her father were in on this from the beginning, and she knew Rowdy was never going to turn up.

He shook his head, recalling the fact that Molly had a solid alibi. She'd been clear across the country when Clay had died and Rowdy had disappeared. But that didn't mean she hadn't had an accomplice here in Fortune Creek. But would that make the partner the killer?

Brandt swore, hating his suspicious nature, hating worse that he had no idea yet who'd killed the ventriloquist or who had Rowdy the Rodeo Cowboy.

Rising from his desk, he plucked his Stetson off the rack and walked out his door, mentally berating himself. Why did he want to suspect Molly?

To keep her at arm's length? Quite possibly, since he'd had his heart broken not all that long ago by a big-city woman. His poor battered heart was still recovering and couldn't be trusted if he got too close to Molly Lockhart.

Attractive or not, Molly was off-limits because her life was in New York City. His life was in Fortune Creek. Not to mention, a very small-town sheriff would be the last man she'd be interested in. Except maybe for a fling with a cowboy. That he'd even consider a short-term romp with the woman had him shaking his head in exasperation. He needed to find Clay's killer and that damned dummy before he did something he would regret.

Molly was visiting with Helen as he came out of his office. Helen was usually a pretty good judge of character, and she seemed to like Molly. He reminded himself that she'd also liked that fluffy bit of fur Ghost too.

"Ready?" he asked at a break in the conversation. He saw both of their startled looks at the abruptness of his tone. He was determined to keep this all business. "Helen, you know where to reach me."

She nodded, her recently permed gray curls bobbing as she turned back to her own desk.

"Helen said you had a burr under your saddle," Molly said after a few miles of silence. "You'll have to translate that for me."

"Wish you'd talked to me about the reward before you offered it," he said without looking at her.

"I thought the idea was to find the murderer."

He looked over at her. "Is it?"

THEY RODE IN silence for a few more miles. Clearly, the sheriff was angry. Just about the reward? Or was there something else bothering him? She thought it might be the latter.

Molly let him stew in his own juices for a while longer before she said, "It was Georgia's idea. She would have offered the reward even if I hadn't offered to pitch in. She has the most to lose if Rowdy isn't found."

"What about you?" he asked, flicking a glance at her before quickly turning back to his driving down the narrow two-lane road. "You seem to have everything to gain by Rowdy *not* being found."

"Is that what's bothering you?" she asked with a laugh as she leaned back against the seat to stare out at the pine trees and mountains that blurred past outside the patrol SUV. Overhead white whisps of clouds skated across the big blue sky. "It's beautiful here." Maybe it was the surprise she too heard in her voice that made him slow down and look at her again.

"You just now noticed that?"

In the hours since his call about her father's

death, she'd felt nothing but angry and inconvenienced, her emotions at war. Look how long it had taken for her to even notice how handsome the sheriff was. No surprise that she hadn't really appreciated the scenery. Or the lawman next to her.

Those blue eyes seemed to search her face as if he could find answers to his suspicions hidden there. Broad-shouldered, slim-hipped with long legs, everything about him sculpted in muscle, how could she not appreciate the view? Like his suntanned hands gripping the wheel. Hands of a working man. She wondered what he'd done before he'd climbed behind the desk as sheriff.

He was nothing like the men she'd dated in New York. Everything about him was strong and capable in this part of the country where such attributes could save your life. Not to mention determined, this man of the law. All of it made him more attractive than any man she'd ever known.

"What?" he asked still sounding irritated. She shook her head. He dragged his gaze away, slowing further to make the turn onto the country road into the Crandell Ranch.

She took a breath, let it out slowly, the cab of the patrol SUV seeming a little too cozy, a little too intimate. What was it about this cowboy that drew her, that made her want to know him and his secrets?

He hit a bump in the road and she wrestled her

thoughts away from the sheriff as she prepared for her father's apparent family. Definitely not welcoming last time. She hated to think how much worse it could be this time.

As she glanced over at the sheriff again, she saw his shoulders tense as he turned down the even more narrow, bumpy road to the ranch. He too was concerned about the reception they would get. She told herself that the Crandells wouldn't shoot the sheriff. At least she hoped not as she saw the buildings ahead—and that huge tree with her father's name carved into it.

BRANDT BRACED HIMSELF as he pulled into the Crandell ranch yard again. He expected this time was going to be more confrontational. It was no secret that the Crandells didn't like visitors; they *really* didn't like the law.

But he was pretty sure the old man had lied about not knowing who Clay Wheaton was. Not that Brandt thought asking about Seth Crandell's murder was going to get him far either. At least he might be able to find out if they knew Seth had a daughter. Maybe they wouldn't care. He supposed it would depend on how they'd felt about their son Seth, he told himself.

"I want you to stay in the patrol car this time." He parked, shut off the engine and turned to her. "This could go a number of ways. If it goes completely south, lock the doors and get on the radio for help. Just push that button."

Her eyes widened in alarm. "Whatever you do, don't get out." As he opened his door, she grabbed his arm to stop him. He looked back at her, seeing her concern for him and smiling even as he told himself not to make too much of it. The drive here had been difficult enough. He'd never been so aware of a woman or his growing curiosity about her.

"It's okay," he said, sorry he'd scared her. "People seldom shoot a sheriff." She slowly released her hold on him and nodded, not looking the least convinced. He wasn't all that certain either.

He climbed out and closed the door before he headed toward the house. He hadn't gone far when the front door flew open.

The elderly rancher they'd seen the last time came out, the same shotgun in his hands, an even more irritated glowering warning on his face. "I thought I told you—"

"Cecil Crandell?" Brandt said. "I don't want trouble. I just need to talk to you about your son Seth."

"Never heard of him. Unless you have a warrant, you'd best get back in that rig and be on your way." He shifted the shotgun, definitely looking like he meant business.

"Put down the shotgun, Cecil. I'm investigating Seth's murder. I just need to ask you a few questions. We can do it here or at the sheriff's department."

"I don't know anything about it," the old man said lowering the shotgun only a hair. "Now get off my property."

With a silent curse, Brandt heard the door of the patrol SUV open behind him. He wanted to throttle Molly. He should have known she wouldn't follow directions.

"You aren't Seth's father?" she demanded. "Well, his DNA says otherwise," she said as she marched toward the house. "If you don't care that he's dead, then you probably don't care that I'm his daughter and a Crandell. *Your granddaughter.*"

Cecil Crandell stared at Molly, eyes hard and narrowed. "I don't care who you are. You're not welcome here."

Brandt started to go after Molly but stopped when the door behind the man opened on a creaky hinge and an elderly woman stepped out drying her hands on her worn apron.

"Who did you say you are?" the woman demanded.

"Go back inside, Irma. I'm handling this," Cecil said.

She ignored him, stepping to the edge of the porch to motion to her granddaughter. Molly moved closer, even though Brandt wanted to pull her back.

"You resemble him," she said, eyes squinted, her voice breaking. "What's your name?"

"Molly." She moved to the edge of the porch.

"Irma, don't make me—"

"Hush, Cecil, you old fool." Her gaze was fixed on Molly. "Come inside." She motioned to Molly, then shot a look at the sheriff. "You stay where you are." Turning to her husband, she said, "Cecil, you see to that tractor of yours. I want to talk to her alone."

For a moment, Brandt held his breath, afraid of what would happen next.

He didn't like the idea of Molly going into that house alone with the woman, but he also had heard clearly in the older woman's voice that he wasn't invited.

Cecil looked as if ready to put up an argument.

The sheriff, realizing how quickly this could go south, gave Cecil a way out. "I'll wait by my patrol car, as long as you promise me this young woman is safe."

Irma Crandell scoffed at even the idea of Molly not being safe in her home. Motioning to her granddaughter, she turned and headed back inside. Over her shoulder, she said, "And put that shotgun down, Cecil."

As Brandt returned to stand next to his patrol SUV, Cecil set down the shotgun, but he didn't go see to his tractor. Instead, he sat down on the porch in a weathered rocker, the weapon within reach.

Brandt didn't like anything about this, but under the circumstances, there wasn't much he could do. He had no evidence that these people had anything to do with Clay Wheaton's death so there would be no chance of getting a warrant. And he sure as hell didn't have any control over Molly Lockhart.

Chapter Ten

Out of the corner of her eye, Molly had watched Cecil as if he was a snake coiled up to strike. He'd leaned the shotgun against the house, but not before she'd seen his fingers shaking with fury.

She'd been almost relieved to get past him and inside the cold and dark old house. It didn't feel that much safer. Shadows seemed to hunker behind the large worn furniture. Irma Crandell led her back through the living room, down a long hallway and finally into the massive ranch kitchen. She followed the woman and the smell of boiled cabbage, her heart in her throat. She'd taken a chance, one the sheriff would be furious about, but she had to know more about her father.

If the information the sheriff had gotten on the DNA was correct, this jerky-tough, scrawny woman had given birth to him. Molly figured Irma Crandell had to be eighty but looked much older as if weathered by her hard life. As they traveled through the old house, Molly had tried to imagine her father growing up here with Cecil and Irma as his parents.

Irma motioned her toward a chair at the kitchen table and went back to her cooking at a huge old stove. "Tell me about Seth," the woman said, her back to Molly.

She had come here hoping to find out about her father—not to fill his mother in on the past half century. On shaky legs, she lowered herself into a chair. "I didn't know he was Seth Crandell." She waited for a reaction; getting none, she continued. "He'd changed his name to Clay Wheaton and became a ventriloquist."

The woman stiffened, then turned, clearly surprised. "One of them fellas that throw their voice to make a doll talk?"

Close enough, Molly thought, and nodded. "After he came out of the military and married my mother, he worked for a while as a mechanic before he became a ventriloquist. I was nine when he left my mother and me. I didn't know anything about his past."

Irma turned back to the stove. "How'd you find us then?"

She took another shaky breath, let it out. "My father came to Fortune Creek, to the hotel there and was murdered." No response. "When they ran his DNA, I discovered his real name and his connection to you. I thought he must have come back here to see you." Still no response. "I was hoping you could tell me about him since I know nothing about the first seventeen years of his life."

Irma lifted a lid on a pot, stirred and put down the spoon. She seemed to slump against the stove for a moment. Molly started to reach for her, afraid she might collapse, but the woman quickly caught herself and turned, wiping her hands on her apron again.

"He was a good boy, so sweet, so gentle," Irma said, her blue eyes filling. "Cecil…" She shook her head. "Seth didn't fit in here on the ranch. It was hard on Cecil even before…" She stopped, swallowed, looked away. "Before the trouble in town, before Seth had to leave."

"What kind of trouble in town?" Molly asked, her voice almost a whisper as the pots on the stove boiled and burbled, the only sound in the room.

"That girl." She waved a hand through the air as if to silence herself. "Where did my son live?"

"I don't know. I lost track of him. I was born in New York City. That's where I still live. I'm a financial analyst. I help businesses invest their money." She saw the woman's blank look along with absolutely no interest in her granddaughter's career. She tried not to let that hurt. What had she expected? Open arms? Any kind of recognition at all?

She refused to let this woman's lack of interest in her hurt her any more than her father's already had. After all, this woman and that man out on

the porch had raised her father. Maybe the sheriff
was right. Maybe her father could only commu-
nicate through a dummy after being raised here
in this house.

"What girl?" she asked.

Irma shook her head. "Not diggin' up that old
bone." She turned back to her stove. "New York
City huh?" she mumbled under her breath before
she said, "You should go. I wouldn't come back
here if I was you."

Molly rose, studying her grandmother's years-
hardened brittle frame for a few moments before
she headed for the door. On the porch, she passed
her grandfather, watching him from the corner of
her eye as she tried not to show fear. She walked,
head high, to the patrol SUV where the sheriff
stood waiting for her. She wasn't going to let these
people get to her.

"Next time I come out here, Cecil, it will be
with a warrant," the sheriff said. Without another
word, they both climbed in. The sheriff started
the engine and drove down the road out of the
Crandell Ranch. Molly felt a strange numbness,
remembering something her mother used to say
when she asked about her father.

Sometimes you don't want to know the truth.

BRANDT COULDN'T BEGIN to guess what had happened inside that house. He mentally kicked himself for letting Molly go in alone—even as he

knew he couldn't have stopped her. Nor, he reminded himself, Cecil would never have allowed him in the house—not without a warrant. He suspected in the past this family had had other run-ins with the law and mentally made a note to check.

Glancing at Molly, he tamped down his anger knowing it rose from his worry about her because of the reckless, dangerous things she did. If anything, he felt a rush of sympathy. Whatever had happened in that house, it hadn't been healing. Her father murdered, her lack of a relationship with him and now finding out that she was the granddaughter of those people back there who he suspected didn't give a whit about her.

He couldn't imagine what she was going through. He tried to read her mood as he drove. She'd just met her grandparents. Not the reunion she'd hoped for, he would bet on that. She couldn't have expected much given Cecil's reaction. Hard to tell with Irma, but something told him that Molly wasn't going to be invited back anytime soon. He gave her time to process it, not pushing, not scolding her for doing exactly what he told her not to do.

"Okay, that was weird," Molly said as they reached the main road. She seemed to shake herself as if throwing off whatever had happened inside that house.

"Are you all right?" he asked, worried about

what that old woman might have told her, even as he reminded himself that he had tried to protect her from her family.

She looked over at him. "Aren't you going to yell at me for getting out of the vehicle, Sheriff?"

"Would it do any good?"

"No."

"Then I guess not. Learn anything interesting a sheriff should know?"

"All she told me was that Seth never fit in on the ranch—Cecil was disappointed in him even before he got into trouble with some girl in town. I'm assuming she meant Eureka—isn't that the closest town?"

He nodded. "What kind of trouble?"

"'*Not diggin' up that old bone*,' Irma said and then told me I shouldn't come back to the ranch again. I suspect if she'd been disappointed in her son before, she was more so now. Apparently, she isn't a fan of New York City nor of ventriloquism."

Brandt chuckled, relieved that Molly seemed to be taking the rejection well enough. At least on the surface. She'd felt rejected by her father and now her grandparents. He wished there was more he could do. But there were things he couldn't protect her from. Maybe herself especially.

"If one of the family killed him," Molly said. "Irma didn't know about it. I got the impression she hadn't even known he was in the area. But if she finds out who killed her son…well, I think she might hurt them. I got the feeling she loved my father and that she blames Cecil for him leaving."

She turned to look at him, determination burning like tears in her eyes. "I want to dig up that old bone and find out why my father was sent away."

CECIL CAREFULLY PUT his shotgun just inside the door where he always kept it and walked into the kitchen. Irma didn't acknowledge him as she set the table.

"You want me to call everyone in for lunch?" he asked. After all these years, he knew this woman better than he knew himself. Just by the set of her narrow slightly stooped shoulders he knew she was furious with him.

She stepped to the flatware drawer, jerked it open and pulled out a large carving knife before she responded. "Did you see him?"

The question hung in the air. He studied her grip on the knife, the way her arthritic fingers clutched it until her knuckles turned white. A lie caught in his throat. "Seth?"

She turned then, knife in hand as she leveled her gaze on him, her warning as clear as the sharp point of the blade. The intensity of her look scared him. Seth had always been her favorite. She'd coddled that boy, and they'd fought about it endlessly until he'd left. Even after what had happened, she'd tried to stop him from signing the papers so the boy could go into the military, saying he was too young, too gentle. Cecil had hoped the army would toughen the boy up, make a man out of him.

What Irma hadn't understood was that Seth had to go and not just because Cecil couldn't bear the sight of his oldest son and she knew it. Her heart had hardened against him the moment he'd signed the papers that would send Seth into the armed service. Then he'd walked out, turning his back on the two of them as he'd silently hoped never to lay eyes on Seth again.

"He was murdered at the hotel in Fortune Creek," she said, her voice raspy and yet controlled. Too controlled.

He shook his head slowly, the lie coming easily at the mere memory of his son, a grown man, with that ridiculous doll. Making the puppet talk and sing, mocking him, mocking his way of life.

"Murdered?" He slumped into a chair and put an arm over his eyes. He could feel her watching him, almost feel the initial prick of the blade before he imagined the lethal, life-ending pain as the knife was plunged into him. He could see how badly she wanted to end this. He just hoped she would go for his heart, puncture it and let him bleed out here in this house, here on this ranch that had been his life.

Time seemed suspended. He couldn't bear to look into her eyes for fear she would see the truth, and nothing could stop her from what he knew she had wanted to do for years.

"You'd best call the boys in," she said dropping the knife back in the drawer and slamming it.

Chapter Eleven

Cecil left the house feeling the weight of Irma's fury over him pushing Seth out settle familiarly on his shoulders. He blamed himself for letting her ruin that boy. He should have stepped in sooner when he saw her mollycoddling Seth. By the time he tried to take the boy in hand, it was too late.

He shuddered at the memory of the man Seth had become. He still couldn't believe him with that puppet on his arm—let alone the words that had come out of that creature's mouth. As if Cecil hadn't known it was his son saying those painful words, pretending the dummy was doing the talking.

Balling his hands into fists, he recalled his rage. He'd wanted to stomp that ridiculous doll into sawdust and lock his hands around his son's throat until he strangled the life from him. Why he had ever agreed to meet Seth after all these years was beyond him. He would regret it the rest of his life. If Irma ever found out…

And now Seth's daughter was in town asking a lot of questions, stirring the pot.

His son Gage came out of his house on the property before Cecil could call out to him. Gage's sons Cliff and Wyatt appeared next to him on the porch, making it clear that they had been watching the goings-on next door even before his son spoke.

"What was that about?" Gage asked. He sounded worried. Cecil wanted to tell him not to concern himself. "I thought you ran that sheriff off?"

Gage was the middle son of the three Cecil had been blessed with. He was thankful for Gage since Seth had been a huge disappointment and Ty... He didn't like to think about Ty who was buried up on a rise behind the house.

If it hadn't been for Gage and his two sons, Cliff and Wyatt, Cecil didn't know how they would have survived and kept the ranch going.

"Nothing to worry about. I'll take care of it," Cecil said and motioned them away from their house and away from their nosey wives inside. "Let's talk on the way over to lunch," he said. Every day, he had Irma make lunch for the boys so they could get back to work without a lot of female prattle at the table from their wives.

He wondered how much they'd witnessed of the sheriff and the young woman. Better to hear it from him than some fool at the feed store. Something like Seth's daughter showing up around here was bound to go countywide if not further. Still it made him angry. He didn't like anyone knowing his business, maybe especially his family.

"It's about that murder over in Fortune Creek."

"Why would the sheriff be asking you about that?" Gage sounded suspicious. Or worried, he wasn't sure which.

Cecil swore, stopping halfway between the houses to get this settled. He couldn't have them talking about any of it in front of Irma. "The man called himself Clay Wheaton." He saw that they'd already heard.

"He was one of them who could throw his voice," Wyatt said nodding. "Had this doll he called Rowdy who could sing. My friend Huck showed me on YouTube. Damnedest thing I ever saw. The man's mouth didn't even move."

"If you're through," Cecil snapped. "He weren't really Clay Wheaton. He made that up. His real name was…" He took a breath and let it out. "Seth. Seth Crandell."

Both of Gage's sons looked confused until their father said, "He was my older brother."

"I thought you said he died in the war," Cliff said.

Seth's name hadn't been spoken for more than half a century on this ranch. There were no photos of him in the house. The carving on the old tree trunk was the only sign that Seth had ever existed.

"What about that girl?" Wyatt asked. "The one who went in the house?"

Cecil growled under his breath. "Seth's daughter. She needs to go back from where she come from before she stirs up more trouble. Now I don't want to hear another word about any of this in front of Irma. She's upset enough. One word and—"

"Understood," Gage said as Cecil gave his grandsons a look that made them snap their mouths shut. "Too bad you can't shut up everyone in the county when this comes out."

Cecil grunted, wishing the same thing. He could feel Gage's questioning gaze on him as if he knew there was more and when it came out...

He knew only too well what it would mean if Irma learned even half of the truth.

In the meantime, he couldn't have Seth's progeny showing up here again. The question was what to do about Molly Lockhart. He considered what it would take to get rid of her like he had her father all those years ago. Whatever he decided, he knew he'd have to do it himself—and without Irma finding out.

BRANDT KEPT THINKING about what Molly had told him regarding Seth getting into trouble with some girl in town. While it might be what had sent him away from the ranch, the sheriff suspected it wasn't the reason Seth Crandell had come home.

But it very well could be what had gotten him killed. It was definitely a place to start by looking into Seth's past. Fortunately, Molly wanted answers as well.

"We could go on into Eureka and ask around about your father at the high school," he said as the patrol SUV idled at the crossroads. Normally, he wouldn't take a civilian on a murder investigation. But her wanting to know about her father would open doors to them that a badge wouldn't. Also, he felt the need to keep an eye on her. He had no idea what she might do next.

"Thought we could stop by the schools, see if anyone remembers Seth or some incident with a town girl about forty years ago," he continued when she didn't answer. "I know it's a long shot, but afterward I'll spring for an elk burger at Trappers."

She nodded as he started to turn left onto the highway toward the small tourist town rather than right toward Fortune Creek. His cell phone rang. It was JP from the coroner's office. "I need to take this." Pulling over to the side of the dirt road, he climbed out of the patrol SUV and walked up the road a way before he answered the call. He didn't want Molly hearing what he knew JP was calling about.

"I was just finishing up the autopsy," the coroner said. "You want to wait until I type up my report?"

"No, what've you got?"

"He appears to have been killed execution style. Shot in the back of the head. The bullet went into his brain. He would have died before he hit the floor."

"The other guests at the hotel said they heard a loud thud as he hit the floor. But they said nothing about a gunshot."

"He was killed with a .22 caliber handgun. Close range aimed so the bullet entered the brain, powerful enough to pierce the skull and then ricochet around inside the cavity scrambling brain matter, but not powerful enough to exit and make a mess. A nice tidy quiet kill."

"A .22?" He couldn't help being surprised.

"Probably something like a Ruger Mark IV, the classic *Hitman* .22 suppressed gun," JP said.

"That's actually the name of the gun?"

"Yep. Short barrel. Anything you put through it would be quieter than the tapping of a pen." The coroner had a fascination with guns after only a few years on the job.

"You're saying the gun probably had a suppressor on it?"

"That would be my guess."

"So the killer would have had to apply for a permit. That should narrow down the suspects," Brandt said. "Also it takes months to get the permit and then the suppressor. He couldn't just buy one at his local convenience store. Clay Wheaton hadn't been in town that long. Unless the killer knew months in advance that the ventriloquist was coming to Montana..."

"There are ways to get around the law. I shouldn't have to tell you that," JP said. "The killer could have already had a weapon with a suppressor on it."

"Okay, let's say the killer got a suppressor for a gun like you mentioned. Clay Wheaton was a big man. The shot was fired at close range, right? So how did he pull that off?"

"It appears the victim was already on his knees. There was no sign of a struggle, but his nose was broken. It appears he fell face forward into the floor and didn't even have a chance to block his fall before he died."

"So there's a good chance that when he opened his hotel room door, he knew his killer."

"Maybe," JP said. "Open the door, someone is holding a gun on you. I suppose you'd do whatever the person said, even get down on your knees. Now what's this about the dummy singing after the ventriloquist died?"

"Pure fantasy."

MOLLY HAD WATCHED the sheriff on the phone in her side mirror. His reaction to whatever news he was getting made her certain it was about her father's murder. She watched him rub the back of his neck, kick at a small rock in the road and shake his head as if he was having trouble believing what he was being told.

She glanced away as he pocketed his phone and headed back to the patrol SUV, a scowl on his handsome face.

"Sorry that took so long," he said as he climbed behind the wheel.

"Something new on my father's murder?" she asked.

He glanced over at her. She saw him debating as to how much to tell her. "It was just the coroner filling me in. I believe we're looking for someone who knew your father and vice versa. Your father didn't put up a fight. Maybe because the killer had a gun on him. Or because he'd been expecting it."

She could tell he was leaving out a lot. "I'll be able to read the coroner's report at some point, right?"

"Once the case is closed," he said. "In the meantime, if it helps, he died instantly." She nodded and looked away as he started the engine. "If you want to go back to the hotel—"

"No," she said quickly. "Let's find out who killed him and took Rowdy."

"Yes, Rowdy. You haven't heard anything from Georgia about the reward offer?"

She shook her head, asking herself why she was going through this. Was it really to get her hands on Rowdy? Or find her father's killer? She suspected it was more complicated than that. She wanted to know her father. But she feared she might regret what she learned after meeting his family. *Her* family, she reminded herself as they left the pine-covered mountains to drop down into the valley.

Eureka in the daylight was like a metropolis compared to Fortune Creek, Molly realized. The other evening it was already dark as they'd entered town. She hadn't gotten a feel for its size. Nor had she realized how close it was to Canada. She saw a sign that said it was only nine miles to the border. She'd never been this far north in the US before. It gave her an odd feeling of being untethered from the world she had known.

With mountain peaks in the distance, she felt strangely more closed in here than in the sheriff's small hometown of Fortune Creek deep in the mountains and trees.

"Is this where you went to high school?" Molly asked as he turned off Highway 93, also known as Dewey Avenue apparently, and drove a block to the school.

"Yep. Good old Lincoln High," he said as he parked in the lot and turned to her. "Here's how I think we should play this. We're inquiring about your father, Seth Crandell. As far as we know, few people know Seth was Clay Wheaton since we just found out. People might be more anxious to talk about Seth under those circumstances."

She nodded. "Unless they're the killer."

"Yep," he said as they entered the high school. It smelled like every high school Molly had ever been in. As they walked down the hallways, she tried to see the sheriff here as a teenager. They passed a glass case with trophies. She slowed, noticing the names engraved on them.

"You were a jock," she said, surprised that she was surprised. It was no shock Ash at the hotel had been a football player. She studied the trophies. "Rodeo?"

"It is Montana," he said and pointed down another hallway. "Come on."

Still she lingered a little longer getting a sense of the teenager he'd been—not all that much different from the man now wearing the badge, she decided. Grinning, she let him lead her deeper into the school. "I'm betting girls just flocked to your rodeos."

"Don't start," he said looking embarrassed. "I was young."

"Young and obviously good at riding anything that bucked."

He shook his head at her as he stopped at a door marked Administration.

"I see you didn't have any trouble remembering where to find the principal's office. You ever get called down here?"

He grinned in answer as he pushed open the door. An older woman looked up from behind the counter. Her eyes widened as she cried, "Brandt? I thought you'd had enough of this school years ago."

He laughed as she came around the counter to give him a hug. "Good to see you, Elsie."

"So you weren't all that bad," she whispered as Elsie went to see if the principal was free.

"It's all relative, but I don't miss this place. I have friends who want to do it all over again. Not me." He glanced at her. "What about you?"

"High school?" She cringed. "Once was plenty. When your father is a ventriloquist, well, a lot of people think it's funny and kids can be cruel."

"I'm sorry."

She waved it off. "I think I've heard every ventriloquist joke there is and some even I was impressed with."

"Still, that had to be hard."

"Clearly, I have some issues when it comes to my father and Rowdy," she said with a laugh. "But I'm working through them."

He gave her hand a quick squeeze before Elsie returned and said they could go in. As they did, the sheriff put his hand on the middle of her back. Even through her jacket, she felt the heat of his touch and missed it as the principal rose from his desk to extend a hand to Brandt.

Principal Hugh Griffith was a robust man with thinning hair and a florid round face. There was a large Stetson on one end of his desk and Molly would bet he was wearing boots. She'd seen rodeo awards in the case alongside Brandt's with that name.

"Brandt, it's almost like yesterday." His smile

was genuine as he greeted them, shaking his friend's hand.

"Good to see you, Hugh," the sheriff agreed. "This is Molly Lockhart. She's staying up in Fortune Creek."

"Nice to meet you. Sit," Hugh said and plopped back into his chair. "And she wanted a tour of your old high school?" He lifted a brow in question.

"Not exactly. She just found out that her father's family is from around here. She was hoping to find out more about Seth Crandell."

"Seth?" He frowned. "Before my time. Any idea when he graduated?"

"He might not have. Joined the military at seventeen."

Hugh turned to his computer. "Give me some idea of when he should have graduated."

Brandt did the math. Seth died at sixty-two. "Forty-five years ago."

"Hmm. I show he was a student, but that's about all I can tell you," Hugh said. "Doesn't look like he participated in any school activities outside of class. You know who might remember him is Walter Franks over at the newspaper. Might even be something in the archives."

IRMA CRANDELL KEPT thinking about that snip of a woman who'd come looking for answers about her father. Molly, she'd called herself. Had some highfalutin job in New York City. Just the kind of

young woman Cecil would find contemptuous—
much like he had her father.

That was why she'd sent her away, telling her
not to come back. She couldn't let Cecil get near
that young woman. Look how he'd been with Seth.
She wasn't going to let her husband destroy Seth's
daughter as well.

Seth. For years she'd done her best to put her
son from her thoughts. It hurt too bad. She'd gone
through the years simply putting one foot in front
of the other, making meals, doing what had to be
done. If she had let him consume her thoughts, she
couldn't have managed. It had been hard enough
to crawl into bed each night next to Cecil, let alone
let him touch her.

But now that she knew Seth had come back,
that Cecil had met with him and lied to her about
it… She found herself filled with a different kind
of fiery rage that she couldn't extinguish. At the
heart of it was the fear that Cecil had killed her
son.

If he had, there was only one thing she could
do, something she regretted not doing all those
years ago. Now she just needed to dig up those
old bones, a truth that had been buried in a deep,
dark hole because she'd been afraid of it coming
to light.

Irma was no longer afraid of facing the past.
It was her present that terrified her to her aging
heart. She thought of Seth's daughter. Her grand-

daughter. She couldn't let sentiment stop her as she planned what to do.

Nothing—and no one—could stop her once she made up her mind.

And her mind had been made up a long time ago.

BRANDT DIDN'T HOLD out much hope in discovering what had happened when Seth Crandell was seventeen. It was as if he was a ghost who'd left no footprint of his years in the area.

The newspaper office was housed in a narrow brick building on the edge of town that looked as if it had been built at least a hundred years ago. Walter Franks, a man about her father's age, explained that both employees were at lunch, but that he would be happy to help.

They sat down after he cleared a stack of newspapers off the chairs in his small office. "Of course, I remember Seth," he said. "Small class especially back then, you know." He rubbed his chin with his fingers as he looked to the ceiling. "Quiet, stayed to himself. He had one friend though who he spent time with I believe—at least at Bud Harper."

"Is Bud still around?" Brandt asked.

Walter shook his head. "Passed a couple of years ago. But Bud's sister still lives here, Lucy Gunther. She might remember something about

Seth. Sorry I can't be more helpful. Whatever happened to Seth?"

"He passed away," Molly said. "I realized I knew very little about him."

Walter had to take care of a customer, but he led them back to a room where they could go through papers from that time on microfiche. They started with the year before Seth Crandell had left for the military.

"It would help if we knew what we were looking for," Molly said. "I haven't found his name anywhere. Apparently, he wasn't involved in any sports or events that might have gotten his name in the newspaper."

Brandt had noticed the same thing. "Some ranchers don't let their sons play school sports because they're needed back home for chores. Seth could have been one of them."

"Did you know Ruby Sherman?" Molly asked.

Her question surprised him. "She's kind of a cautionary tale around these parts," he said distractedly as he looked through old papers.

"There's a big long article about her car wreck. I wonder if my father knew her. They were about the same age."

Brandt was ready to give up when Molly said, "Here's something. 'Ty Crandell, son of Cecil and Irma Crandell, died of a gunshot wound.' That's all it says other than his death was being investigated. But it's dated...forty-five years ago. That would have been the year my father left for the service."

Brandt glanced over at the short article. "You're right. My father was sheriff back then," he said looking at the date of Ty's death. "There might be something in the case file. I'll check." He sighed. "Are you up to trying to locate Lucy Gunther while we're in town? Maybe we should have lunch first."

"I'm not very hungry."

His cell phone rang. He excused himself and took the call. "JP, you have something for me?" He listened. "Okay, on my way." He disconnected. "I need to get back."

"It's fine with me. I'm anxious to find out if there's been any response to the reward Georgia posted and I haven't been able to reach her by phone."

"Sure," he said, seeing the fatigue on her face. The more they found out, the more it appeared that Seth Crandell wasn't even a ghost. It was as if he'd never existed—at least not in any memorable way. "Let me know if you get a response on the reward."

MOLLY NODDED, wondering how she and Georgia would handle the exchange if someone did come forward—especially knowing the person could be a killer.

As the sheriff drove them out of Eureka and into

the mountains toward Fortune Creek, she closed her eyes, suddenly feeling exhausted. Just that morning she'd met her grandmother and grandfather. It was hard not to be insulted by their lack of interest in her. Irma had acted as if she'd loved her son, that he might have been a favorite and yet she'd had no interest at all in his daughter.

The apple hadn't fallen far from the tree, she reminded herself. Her own father hadn't had any trouble cutting her from his life, preferring to spend all his time with Rowdy. She wondered if she would ever find out who Seth Crandell had been, this man behind the puppet—or if she wanted to.

The next thing she knew she was bolting awake lost in more of a nightmare than a dream, her seat belt keeping her from flying to her feet. She frantically looked around, unsure where she was. The sheriff, she saw, had pulled up in front of his office and shut off the engine. That must have been what had awakened her.

She'd fallen asleep?

"You all right?" he asked in concern.

She nodded even though she was still partially trapped in the nightmare, trapped in the Crandell kitchen with Cecil saying something about killing a bad gene. She shivered as the nightmare began to disperse like fog burning off in sunshine.

Her mouth dry, her pulse still thumping, she reached to open her door. She was anxious to get out, needing fresh air and both feet on the ground to assure her that she wasn't still in that nightmare about to die.

"Thank you for taking me along," she said as he climbed out on the other side. She looked across the hood of the SUV at him. He had that worried frown on his face. "I appreciate everything you're doing for me."

"I'm also looking for his killer," he reminded her. "But I'm glad I can help you as well."

She felt foolish. Of course, he hadn't done this all because of her. He was merely doing his job; their two agendas, if not exactly the same, were close enough that they could help each other. Flushing with embarrassment, she turned and hurried across the street to the hotel.

In the lobby, she saw that Ash wasn't behind the desk and was relieved. She wasn't in the mood for chitchat. Strands of that strange dream rolled in on the mist fogging her brain. She took the elevator, glad she didn't have to share it. She wondered if she and Georgia were the only guests in this place. The thought wasn't a comforting one.

At Georgia's door, there was no response to her knock. She tried again, then turned to her own room. After she unlocked her door, it swung open and she saw that someone had left her a note. It was on hotel stationery, a single sheet folded in half. It had apparently been slipped under her door.

Georgia, she thought as she picked it up. Had

someone contacted them about Rowdy? Stepping in, she dropped her purse on the bed and unfolded the single sheet of hotel stationery.

Her hand began to shake as she blinked down at the childishly large handwriting randomly placed across the page. It took her a moment to figure out what it even said, especially with the numerous ink blotches that had spilled on the page.

Her heart leaped to her throat as the words suddenly made sense.

It was a ransom note.

Chapter Twelve

The sheriff had just returned to his office when he got the call. He ran across the street, having told Molly not to handle the note more than she already had, and to stay where she was.

He took the stairs to the fourth floor rather than ride up in the slow, antiquated elevator. He was breathless before he reached her room and knocked. She opened the door at once.

"Are you all right?" she asked as he leaned on the doorframe for a moment trying to catch his breath.

"I ran up the stairs, three at a time," he said between breaths. "Where's the note?"

She pointed to the bed where she'd apparently dropped it. Pulling out the gloves and evidence bag from his pocket, he approached the bed. The note lay open on the quilt covering. Just as she'd said, it was on hotel stationery.

What she hadn't mentioned, though, were the ink spots. He would have to compare them to the note Clay Wheaton had left before he was killed, but Brandt was sure they were going to match. The killer had taken the stationery and the leaky pen. Already planning to write a ransom note?

The note was difficult to read. The person writing it had tried, it appeared, to hide his or her handwriting so it wouldn't be recognized. Did that mean it was someone he knew, someone whose writing he would have known?

Whoever had written this hadn't known about the leaky pen, but they'd definitely been in Clay Wheaton's room—or someone they knew had been. If they had paid attention to the note Clay Wheaton had left on the bureau for his contacts, they might have noticed that the pen had leaked.

Was this from the murderer? It certainly could be. Didn't they realize how incriminating this was? Were they trying to get caught for his murder?

He couldn't shake the feeling that this note had been written by someone close to the killer—but not the killer himself. Someone who now had the hotel stationery and the pen. But did they also have Rowdy?

He shook his head. "I'm still trying to connect the dots—no pun intended," he said.

"He wants five thousand dollars," Molly told him as she joined him next to the bed.

Brandt could see that. Had whoever left this heard about the reward and figured the dummy was worth five times that amount? Or had the writer of the ransom note just picked a random number?

"I'll pay it." She sounded stronger than earlier, more determined. Her nap on the way home in the patrol SUV must have done her good.

"We can't know for sure that this person even has Rowdy," he said, then looked at Molly, studying her. "You want the dummy that badly?"

"I want the killer that badly," she corrected. "I can't imagine growing up in that house where my father was raised or why he would ever come back here. I want answers, but I also want justice."

He wanted to tell her that justice was illusive and often unsatisfying. It was seldom an easy thing to get. If Seth Crandell had done something that had made him flee here, join the military, change his name and never return—until recently—then justice might have already been meted out by the killer. Montana was famous for vigilante justice from back in the state's Wild West beginnings.

"The person wants us to bring the money tomorrow night to a spot in the woods." He shook his head. "Even if we were going to pay it, there isn't any way you could put together that much cash in such a short time."

"I can. At least I can try."

He turned to stare at her. "You do realize this could be a shakedown and that this person doesn't have Rowdy, never did."

"Or the person does because he was in my father's room that night after killing him, found Rowdy and took the case with the dummy inside."

Brandt was shaking his head again. "The first thing we need to know is who dropped off this note. Hopefully we can get a decent print off the paper." The person had been in the hotel, had known what room Molly was staying in and had left without being seen? He quickly called down to the desk. It rang four times before a winded Ash picked up.

Brandt recalled that Ash hadn't been at the desk when he'd rushed past. "Where have you been?"

"Brandt? I was down at the café getting something to eat. I still have to eat you know."

"Sorry. How long do you think you were gone?"

"Seriously?" A sigh. "Twenty, twenty-five minutes. But it wasn't like I couldn't see down the main drag if someone had pulled in and wanted a room."

"Is that the only time you've been away from your post?" the sheriff asked.

"Except for a quick bathroom break. What's this about?"

"Never mind." He disconnected and turned to Molly. "Ash was away from the hotel. Anyone could have come in and shoved the note under your door. Anyone who knew what room you were in."

"You're that sure the note was for me?" she asked. "I wasn't the one who posted the reward."

He nodded, before he placed another call. Helen answered right away. "Any chance you might have seen someone going into the hotel especially in the past half hour?"

"I was on my lunch break, watching my stories on my phone," she said. "I wasn't sitting here looking out the window."

He disconnected. It struck him that anyone who knew the routines of this town would have known exactly when to enter the hotel without being seen. "Let's just hope we get a print off the note before we're contacted again."

"You mean when I'm contacted?"

He met her gaze. "Don't even think about not telling me if you get another note."

"Why would I get another one? This could all be over tomorrow night when we meet him in the woods," she said.

He glanced at her. Finding the note had scared her. Now that she was thinking clearly, he figured she was wishing she hadn't told him about the note. "*We* are not meeting him. When no one shows up, the person will get in contact again."

"If the note was left for me, the person knows who I am. I'm the only one who can go to the drop site since it says on the note, *no law*."

If the person who left the ransom note, had purposely put it under her door, then they must know that she was Clay Wheaton's daughter. It was common knowledge in Fortune Creek and after the two of them had been asking questions around Eureka, word could have easily spread.

And then there were the Crandells. They now knew about her. Maybe they'd known Seth had a daughter long before this if one of them had met with the ventriloquist—and killed him—and seen the note with her name and number on it.

"Please don't fight me on this," he said quietly. "I'm just trying to keep you alive." Under all her outrage and determination, Molly looked pale and vulnerable. Damn but he wanted to take her in his arms for all the wrong reasons. His gaze went to her mouth. The desire to kiss her was so strong that he had to make himself keep both feet firmly on the floor. He didn't dare take even one step toward her. She was already so near that he felt as if he could feel the electricity sparking between them. It would take so little to close the distance.

Her gaze locked with his, stealing his breath as he saw the flare of heat in her eyes and realized it wasn't all anger and determination. She felt the heat between them. Her gaze shifted from his eyes to his mouth. Her lips parted as if of their own will. He felt a pull stronger than all his determination and was too aware of the bed next to them. Too aware of this woman.

She'd pried open his closed heart in a way that felt more than dangerous. *You think you got your heart broken last time? This woman could very easily rip it out and stomp the life out of it—right before she drives out of town.*

She blinked and stepped back, either running from the need in his gaze or her own. Then again it could be just simple self-preservation. She wouldn't want to get involved with some small-town sheriff, knowing full well how it would end.

He swallowed, his mouth suddenly dry at the thought of how close he'd come to making a huge mistake with more than his heart. He picked up the bagged ransom note. Molly moved to allow him access to her hotel room door. He headed for it. "Call me when you get the next note."

She didn't answer. She didn't have to. He already knew that she wouldn't. Molly Lockhart thought she could handle this by herself. He swore as he left, practically bumping into Georgia as he closed the door.

MOLLY FELT AS if she'd just dodged a bullet. She was so wired by that tense exchange between her and the sheriff that she jumped at the knock on her door. She was afraid to open it, afraid it would be the lawman and that this time neither of them would call a halt to what had almost happened before. Her heart was still hammering, her blood running hot, desire simmering in places she'd seldom if ever felt before.

"Georgia," she said as she opened the door to

the insurance woman. She felt a wave of relief—
and disappointment that it wasn't the sheriff.

"I thought you might want to go to lunch. Are
you all right?" The woman turned to look back
down the hallway at the sheriff's retreating back.
"Been doing a little entertaining in your room?"
Georgia chuckled as if she was joking, but her
look when she turned back was probing.

"Lunch," Molly said, needing fresh air and to
escape the feelings the sheriff had evoked in her
as well as to get out of her hotel room. Right now,
she would go anywhere Georgia suggested.

"You don't seem all right," Georgia said as they
walked down the hallway to the stairs. "You look
like you've seen a ghost." Her eyes widened. "You
haven't seen a ghost, have you?"

Molly shook her head. "I need air." She turned
toward the fire escape stairs. She knew that the
sheriff wouldn't want her talking to anyone about
the ransom demand, so she couldn't blame that
for her apparent frightened expression. "I met
my grandparents this morning and survived it.
Barely."

She pushed open the door and descended the
fire escape. When they reached the bottom, , they
headed down the alley to the café. "Seriously?
You talked to your grandparents?" Georgia said,
having to trot to catch up with her.

"It was more than strange and a whole lot
disconcerting. My grandfather had his shotgun

loaded the entire time and my grandmother..."
She shook her head. "I think she loved my father.
I don't think she knew he was murdered let alone
that he'd been nearby in Fortune Creek."

"Do you think one of them killed him?" Georgia asked.

"I don't know. I'm not sure I want to know."
Her thoughts kept shifting back to the sheriff, the
heat of his look. She licked her lips unconsciously
and tried to breathe. The last thing she needed
to do was get involved with the cowboy sheriff.
She couldn't trust her emotions right now—even
if he wasn't the sheriff of Fortune Creek, Montana and she didn't live thousands of miles away
in New York City.

Her libido teased her with the thought of a fling.
Except that she didn't do flings and she had a feeling that neither did the sheriff.

Georgia was talking but she was barely listening as she pushed open the door to the café.
"Hey, ladies. I just need to step out for a few minutes," Alice called. "I'm going to run some of my
chicken soup over to May Greenly. She's feeling under the weather I heard. Take a seat. I'll be
right back."

"Okay, something has you spooked and I don't
think it's your weird relatives," Georgia said as
they sat down at a table across from each other.

"Sorry," Molly said, shaking her head as if to
throw off the chill she'd just gotten. "It's my fa-

ther. Finding out that he's Seth Crandell, well, it could mean that a lot of his show with Rowdy was based on things that actually happened to him. It's kind of…spooky to be here and know that he grew up here. He might have known a lot of these people."

Georgia seemed to be waiting as if she knew there was more.

Molly looked toward the back door that Alice had gone out to take soup to her ill neighbor. "That name. May Greenly. It's…familiar. I think I heard Rowdy mention it in one of my father's shows." She frowned, repeating the name under her breath as she tried to remember what Rowdy had said about May.

"Okay, I can see where this would be weird for you. I mean meeting grandparents you never knew you had," Georgia said. "I hate to freak you out more, but we've received five responses to our reward notice. What do you think we should do now?"

Molly stared at her. *Five people claim they have Rowdy?* She sighed, feeling as if she was still in a nightmare. She'd dreamed again last night that she'd heard Rowdy singing. She thought of the ransom demand. Did the five people who responded to the reward know about the ransom demand? Or was someone hoping to double dip. So who was lying about having Rowdy? Maybe all of them—including the ransom demand writer.

"The sheriff was right. This was a mistake. How are we going to do this?"

"All we can do is agree to meet with each one, right?" Georgia was saying. "They all left phone numbers and first names."

Molly shook her head. "I definitely think we should tell the sheriff then. Don't look at me like that. This could be dangerous."

"All five said, 'no cops.'"

"Of course they did. Which is exactly why we need to tell the sheriff. One of them could be the killer."

"No sheriff," Georgia said adamantly. "What makes you think you can trust him anyway? Those dreamy blue eyes? Or the way his jeans fit that perfect bottom of his?"

It annoyed Molly that Georgia had noticed the sheriff's assets. "Very funny. Seriously, I think he knows what he's doing. I…trust him." That surprised her but she realized it was true. "If you want Rowdy back, then he should at least know about the people who contacted you for the reward. There's more going on than you know."

Georgia gave her an impatient look. "Between you and the sheriff?"

"On the murder case. Let's talk to him after lunch, please. You don't want to do anything that might jeopardize getting Rowdy back."

Georgia grudgingly agreed. "Once Rowdy is found, we can go back to our lives."

"Exactly." Even as she said it though, Molly knew that it had gone far beyond that. She wanted to know why someone had killed her father. She thought it might be the key that would unlock everything, including why he couldn't stay with her and her mother all those years ago.

BRANDT HAD JUST gotten off the phone when he saw the two women headed down the street toward his office. He groaned, definitely not in the mood after his call from the crime scene techs who'd processed Clay Wheaton's pickup.

"Got fingerprints and DNA," the tech told him. The sheriff had listened as he was told that both Gage Crandell's and his father Cecil's fingerprints were found in the pickup.

The only surprise was that the prints found on the takeout box found in the truck were Cecil's.

"All this proves is that Cecil and Gage had been in Clay Wheaton's pickup," the sheriff said, thinking out loud. "But it didn't sound like Cecil and his son had been at each other's throats if the older man had enjoyed a piece of Alice's huckleberry pie. Where were their fingerprints found in the pickup?"

"Cecil's on the passenger side door handles. Gage's on door handles and the steering wheel and the gear shift knob."

Brandt had sworn under his breath. "Gage drove the pickup? How did that happen?"

"Good question."

"I'd like to ask him," he'd said, not that he thought he'd get a straight answer even if he could get Gage in for questioning. He swore under his breath.

Since that awkward moment in the hotel room with Molly, he'd come back to work in a funk. He'd thrown himself into his work, tracking down information in his father's old files on Ty Crandell's death.

He'd just been debating finding Molly and telling her what he'd learned. He wasn't sure how Ty's suicide might tie into Seth's leaving Montana for the service, but he had a feeling it might. Ty had killed himself shortly after Seth left.

That's when he'd seen the two women crossing the street making a beeline for his office. Now he braced himself as they entered. He motioned for Helen to let them come on back.

"We've heard on the reward," Molly said the moment she cleared his office threshold.

"Someone says they have Rowdy?" He wasn't sure how to feel about that. They already had a ransom note. Could both be from the same person?

"Five people have responded," Georgia said.

Brandt groaned and motioned for them to sit down. This was exactly what he'd feared, a bunch of wild goose chases that would lead to nothing more than someone trying to make a fast buck.

"What kind of information did they provide to reach them to make the trade?"

Molly and Georgia exchanged a look. He knew that look.

"The reward was Georgia's idea. She's handled it—she has the contacts. I don't. You're going to have to talk to her."

"It isn't something the two of you want to handle on your own," he said feeling his frustration rising. "This is dangerous. There is a murderer out there. He might want the money to skip town. You think he'd leave either of you alive to describe him?"

"I have phone numbers and what could be first names, but they warned us not to go to the sheriff," Georgia pointed out.

"Of course they did," he said. Clearly, Georgia had been against telling him. Which meant Molly must have talked her into it. He glanced at her, relieved one of them was taking this seriously.

He did, however, wonder if Molly had mentioned the ransom note to Georgia. He met her gaze, decided she had kept it a secret. He gave her the hint of a smile before he asked for the phone numbers.

"We're not reckless," Georgia said. "We were going to meet them separately in a public place."

He couldn't help thinking about the ransom demand. Did that person have Rowdy? Or were all of these people trying to cash in?

"The problem is, even if one of them really does have Rowdy, we don't have the cash yet," Molly said.

"Like any ransom demand, they need to prove that they have the dummy first," the sheriff said.

"Like a piece of Rowdy's clothing," Molly suggested.

Georgia turned to stare at her. "Would you recognize a piece of his clothing? I wouldn't."

"Bad idea, sorry."

"I might suggest having each of them text you a photograph of Rowdy in front of this week's *Tobacco Valley News* out of Eureka," the sheriff said.

Molly nodded. "I'll see about getting the money wired here in the meantime."

Brandt lifted a hand. "We need to start by running the phone numbers you were sent and see who's behind the reward demands, if you don't mind me making another suggestion."

Georgia groaned but handed over the list. He quickly checked out the phone numbers she'd been given. One was the main number at the high school office. The name with it was Monte. Another had used the number at a bar in Eureka, name Wild Bill. A third had used the number at the newspaper in Eureka where the reward notification had run, name Hank. Each of those had given a first name to ask for. The fourth had used a burner phone. Only one had used a phone number under his name. He recognized the name of a person he'd had to arrest for a number of infractions over the years.

Brandt swore under his breath and looked at the two women sitting across from him. "Here's what I'd suggest we do."

IRMA CRANDELL WAITED until her husband, Gage and Cliff had gone to the barn to work on the tractor. She found her grandson Wyatt in the butchering room about to cut up the pig he had hanging.

He looked up, surprised to see her. In this family, women's work was inside the house. Everything else fell to the men and wasn't any of the women's business.

"I need to talk to you," Irma said, closing the door. She locked it and turned to see Wyatt's eyes as wide as a harvest moon. "You're going to tell me the truth, aren't you, boy." He nodded looking as if he wanted to make a run for it. "This is just between the two of us. You get my meaning?" Another nod as she took the knife he'd been sharpening away from him. "Tell me everything you know about Seth." She touched the blade of the knife, finding it plenty sharp. *"Everything."*

Then she listened as Wyatt stumbled over the words, his gaze going from her face to the knife in her hand.

When he finished filling her in on what he knew, she asked, "Who killed Seth?"

Wyatt looked like his bladder might fail him

as he said, "I don't know. I swear, I don't." As scared as he looked, she thought he was telling the truth. All she could hope was that he feared her more than his grandfather. She studied him for a full minute before she put down the knife and reached over to cup his face. He was the most like Seth, something she knew her husband would try to kill in him.

The thought filled her with that familiar sense of desolation as she walked to the door and unlocked it. As she swung the door open, she came face-to-face with Cecil.

"Irma? What are you doing down here?" Cecil demanded, looking past her to Wyatt.

"Just telling the boy how I want my pork chops cut this time," she snapped and pushed past him. But as she walked away, she glanced back, catching Wyatt's eye and giving him a warning look.

Chapter Thirteen

"We need to weed out anyone who doesn't have the dummy," the sheriff was saying. Georgia tried each of the numbers, asked for the person whose name she had and then told the person who answered that she would need a photo of the puppet with this week's newspaper texted to her.

He noticed that Molly didn't seem to be listening. "There a problem?"

"Do you know May Greenly?"

He'd been right. She hadn't been listening. Because she wasn't concerned about the calls because she knew none of these people had Rowdy? Or was something else on her mind.

"May Greenly was my third-grade teacher. Why are you asking about her?"

Molly shook her head, motioning for him to move on.

Georgia finished and pocketed her phone. "So now we wait. I left the message for each of the people who contacted us."

Brandt sighed. "If you get a photo of Rowdy

sent to your phone with this week's *Tobacco Valley News* paper, we'll set up a meeting with the person. But I will be the only person going."

"I don't like it," Georgia said. "They spot you and they could get rid of Rowdy."

"First off, I doubt we will hear from any of them. I'd be shocked if one of these people had Rowdy and sent a photo. If you get any more hits on the reward, please treat them the same way. The point is to find Rowdy, right?" Both women nodded. "I'm serious about this being dangerous. Never forget, if you decided to follow up on your own, you could be meeting with the killer."

He didn't really believe that. He thought more than likely it would be the author of the ransom demand who they really had to worry about. But he didn't want Molly and Georgia taking the chance he was wrong.

Georgia got to her feet. She glanced at Molly who was still sitting, gave a shake of her head and walked out.

"Are you all right?" he asked after Georgia had left.

Molly stirred. "No, not really." She plastered on a smile. "I'm fine really." The lie didn't float and she knew it.

He let it go for now. "Thanks for not telling Georgia about the ransom demand you received. We'll handle it the same way once we hear from the alleged kidnapper again." She nodded but he wasn't all that sure she was listening. He reminded himself what she'd been through since arriving in Fortune Creek. She was dealing with a lot, some of it maybe just now hitting home.

As she started to leave, he detained her long enough to reiterate, "Let me know the moment you get another ransom note."

"I won't touch it. I'll call you at once," she said impatiently. "But you're not keeping me out of the loop either. You need me. Seems we need to trust each other."

He sighed as he met her gaze, rose and walked around his desk to her. She was in the driver's seat and they both knew it. From the look in her eyes, he'd pay hell slowing her down once she put her foot on the gas. He was along for what could be a very bumpy ride.

Swallowing, he held out his hand. "You have my word." She took his hand. Warmth spread up his arm as he was quickly reminded of earlier in her hotel room. He felt his pulse jump of its own accord. Desire feathered through him, bringing a rush of heat to places that had been forsaken for some time.

Helen cleared her throat. Brandt realized she'd been standing in the doorway behind Molly apparently for some time. "Two calls for you, Sheriff." There was a warning edge to her tone.

He let go of Molly's hand. "Talk soon," he said, his voice sounding rough with desire even to his ears—and no doubt to Helen's from the way she narrowed her eyes. "I'll take that first call now, Helen," he said pointedly. He knew she was only trying to look out for him. Didn't want him making a fool of himself like he had the last time with a city girl.

Brandt turned to his desk, thankful for the phone calls. Still, after he sat down, he took a moment to catch his breath before he picked up. "Sheriff Parker."

"We didn't get any viable fingerprints off the ransom demand," the tech at the lab informed him. "Wanted to let you know."

He thanked him and told Helen to put through the second call, hoping it would be more productive.

"Sheriff, it's Lucy Gunther returning your call."

He'd forgotten he'd called Bud Harper's sister. "Yes, I was calling about Seth Crandell. I understand he and your brother had been friends."

"Wow, I haven't heard that name in a long time. Seth? Now that I think about it, he and Bud did hang out some in middle school, maybe a little in high school? Didn't Seth drop out, join the service before graduation?"

"He left at seventeen. What can you tell me about Seth and possibly a girl he dated in town?"

"That was so long ago," Lucy said. "I wish Bud was still here. He might remember, but you know, I do have Bud's photo albums. He was always taking snapshots. Why don't I look through them and get back to you."

"Sounds great. Really appreciate this."

"I suppose you can't tell me why you'd be interested in Seth Crandell after all these years."

"Not at this point."

She chuckled. "You have me intrigued. I'll go dig out those albums. There have to be some shots of Seth, I would think."

Brandt hoped so as he thanked her again and hung up. It would seem that Seth had made little mark on the area in his seventeen years. But then again, that would depend on the kind of trouble he'd gotten into with some town girl like Irma Crandell had mentioned.

IRMA MULLED OVER everything her grandson had told her. None of it had come as a surprise. Cecil and Gage had gone to see Seth at the hotel one night late. How they'd known he was there was a mystery to Wyatt. But Irma figured Seth had contacted his father somehow to let him know he was in the area.

Why in the world would Seth be so foolish as to contact the man who'd hated him all those years, she had no idea. That Gage went along to see him gave her hope that her husband hadn't killed Seth—at least not that night.

"You have any idea what they talked about?" she had asked Wyatt who'd said he didn't. They'd come home even later that night, the two men then going their separate ways.

Which meant that all she knew for sure was that her husband was a liar. She had little doubt though that he could also be a killer.

When she'd heard about the reward being offered for the doll Seth used in his show, she'd been shocked at first, then curious. The dummy was missing. If her husband had killed Seth like she feared, then maybe he'd brought the dang thing home. Maybe he'd hidden it, though she couldn't imagine why he would do that.

Still, she had to search for it. The doll would prove what she knew in her heart. Cecil hated his son enough to kill him—and then lie to her face.

MAY GREENLY LIVED in a small cottage behind the café. The house reminded Molly of a gingerbread house found in the woods in a fairytale. There was a flowerpot up front full of marigolds, and cute lace curtains at the windows.

At the pretty turquoise door, Molly stopped, feeling as if she was opening up Pandora's box. But since hearing the woman's name, she hadn't been able to quit thinking that this might be a person from one of Rowdy's stories.

Did she really want to find out more of her father's secrets though? She'd never imagined that he had so many. He'd seemed like a man who had never lived much. Wasn't that why he'd become a ventriloquist—because something was missing? Or because he was hiding behind Rowdy? She felt as if she was close to finding out as she tapped at the door and waited.

It was a beautiful day, the sky so blue that it hurt to look at it. The pine trees gleamed dark green in the sunlight. The air was so clear and clean that she knew she'd never breathed anything like it before. She tapped again recalling what the owner of the café had said. May seldom left her house and she hadn't been feeling well. Molly was about to leave, thinking this wasn't a good time, when she heard movement inside.

A few moments later the door opened and a small gray-haired woman in a wheelchair appeared. No one had mentioned that May was in a wheelchair. Molly feared she should have called or come at another time and said as much.

"Don't be silly," the woman said. Her whole face lit, sparking the blue eyes and taking years from her round face. "Your timing is perfect." May continued to smile, not concerned in the least to have a stranger on her doorstep.

"I'm Molly Lockhart. I was hoping to speak to you about my father."

"Your father?"

"Seth Crandell," she said and saw from the woman's expression that she'd come to the right place. There was something so sweet and innocent in the woman's face. She guessed her to be in her late fifties or early sixties, close to Seth Crandell's age. "You knew my father."

The woman opened the door wider as she wheeled out of the way. "Please, come in. Would you like some tea? Or perhaps some coffee?" she asked as Molly followed her into the kitchen. The walls and shelves were filled with souvenirs from around the country and the world beyond. "No, thank you," Molly said distractedly as she gazed at the souvenirs. "You must have traveled a lot."

May laughed as she offered her a chair at the table. "Oh, no, dear, I've never left Fortune Creek. I lived vicariously through the wonderful things your father sent me."

Molly was about to take a chair at the kitchen table, but stopped in surprise. "My father sent you all of those?"

"You sound surprised," May said as she wheeled up to an empty space at her kitchen table. "He traveled with his show, but surely you know that."

Molly shook her head as she sat. "I don't know very much about my father. He left my mother and me when I was nine."

"I'm so sorry," May said. "That must have been very painful for you and your mother."

"How did you know my father?" She thought of the ventriloquist show she'd watched online. He'd said through Rowdy that May was his sweetheart.

"We grew up together. I was very fond of your father."

"He was very fond of you," Molly said. "At one of his shows, he said you were his sweetheart and that you'd broken his heart." May smiled, but said nothing. "Are you aware that he recently died?" She saw the answer on the woman's face. A sadness seemed to soften her features even more. Tears welled in her eyes.

"Yes, I heard. I was so sorry."

"I have to ask—did you see my father while he was here in Fortune Creek?"

May nodded, smiling. "He came to see me, and we visited just like old times." She looked so happy, as if lost in the memory.

"Did he tell you what he was doing in Fortune Creek?"

"He said he had some unfinished business here," she said. "He came to say goodbye."

"Then he told you he was sick?"

"Yes, I was so sorry to hear it. After everything he'd been through, I hated seeing him in such pain, both physical and mental."

"I'm sorry, you said everything he'd been through?"

May pursed her lips. Sunshine poured in the window and splashed across the kitchen table. She wiped at a speck of dust on the surface with the hem of her sleeve. "I love this room. It's my favorite because of all the light, but it always highlights any dust that I've missed." She chuckled to herself.

Molly could tell that the woman was stalling, not sure of how much she wanted to say. "Please, I would appreciate anything you can tell me about my father. I'm realizing more and more how little I knew about him or how many secrets he had."

"He loved you," May said. "He was so proud of you. He told me how successful you are and how beautiful." She smiled. "He wasn't exaggerating one bit either." The woman was still skirting around the question.

"What happened to make him leave when he was seventeen? I watched one of his shows and he talked about May Greenly being his first love. Of course he told the story through Rowdy."

"Of course, he did," May said laughing. "He and Rowdy traveled the world together. They were so close."

"Rowdy is a dummy, a puppet, not real."

"Are you sure about that?" she asked, a twinkle in her eye. "Rowdy was very real to your father."

"So you saw Rowdy, when my father came to visit."

May laughed. "Of course. He wouldn't have come without Rowdy. I loved them both and enjoyed Rowdy's stories and songs so much."

"You know Rowdy is missing?" Molly asked.

"I was so sorry to hear that. Rowdy had become his best friend. Rowdy was all that he had at the end."

"He had a family, a daughter he could have

turned to, but he obviously chose not to," Molly said, hating the bitterness in her voice.

"I know, it does seem that way. But your father didn't want to burden you with the ghosts from his past, the demons that followed him through life."

"What demons were those?" Molly demanded.

May looked down at her hands in her lap. "You asked why he left at seventeen. I wish I could tell you. It isn't that I don't want to or that I'm keeping secrets for him—I honestly don't know. For so many years I blamed myself for him leaving. We were in love, but we were too young. Even if our families would have agreed to let us marry, we couldn't. As much as I loved your father..." She shook her head. "It wasn't meant to be."

"Did you ever marry?"

"Oh, no, dear," May said. "I never met anyone like your father again. I know it sounds silly, but he was the love of my life. I didn't want anyone else."

"What was my father like when he was young?"

Her face lit up. "He was charming and so sweet and so loving and so generous. He saw beyond my handicap. He saw into my heart."

"Your handicap?"

"I had polio as a child. I've never been able to walk."

Molly stared at her, stunned. "I'm so sorry—I had no idea."

"Please don't feel sorry for me. I've had a wonderful life. Living here in Fortune Creek has been a joy. I have such close friends—it's such a wonderful community. I've always had love."

"There has to be a reason why he left the way he did, why he changed his name, why he was so… unsettled his whole life. Are you sure it wasn't because he was heartbroken that the two of you couldn't be together?"

"We both were heartbroken, but he promised that he would always stay here, that he would always be here if I ever needed him."

"He made that same promise to my mother. Seems he wasn't good at keeping promises." Molly thought about how easily he had walked away from her and her mother. Had he done the same thing to May? Or had something happened that he couldn't stay, that he had to go away and change his name and never be Seth Crandell ever again? "Didn't you ever ask him why he broke his promise to you?"

May shook her head. "I never needed to. I knew your father's heart. He wouldn't have left unless he was forced to. I always thought my family might have threatened him."

"Are any of your family still around?" she had to ask, but the woman shook her head.

"I'm so sorry you never got to know your father. He was a good man, though he had his demons. I never asked what they were. I'm just thankful that now he's at peace." She smiled. "I hope to join him one day. He'll be waiting for me."

Molly hoped so, but she personally wouldn't have counted on that.

CECIL CRANDELL WAS no detective, but it didn't take him long to find out that Molly Lockwood was staying on the same floor at the same hotel her father had in Fortune Creek.

Gage's daughter-in-law had come back from town with the news along with details about the reward. Cecil hadn't seen the ad in the newspaper, because he didn't take the paper, but Cliff's wife had picked it up on one of her many trips into town. Cecil didn't want to get started on how he felt about her constantly leaving the ranch.

"Someone's offering a reward for that doll?" he demanded.

"*A thousand dollars.* Shirley said everyone in the county is looking for that dummy." Gage looked at his father as if hoping Cecil had it.

"Craziest thing I've ever heard," was all Cecil had said and had gone back to work. But it kept nagging at him. A thousand dollars? That puppet doll couldn't be worth a plug nickel. It had to be a trap. The sheriff was hoping whoever killed Seth would try to collect the reward and then he would arrest him. All over some doll dressed like a cowboy.

Just the thought of that puppet and his son had

him so worked up by that evening that he could barely eat. Right after dinner, he left without a word, got into his truck and drove off the ranch.

He'd seen Irma's face as he was leaving. She'd been watching him lately after years of not even looking in his direction. He had to put an end to this before things got out of hand.

Chapter Fourteen

Molly sat straight up in bed, her heart racing. Darkness. She hadn't been able to sleep earlier and was surprised that she'd fallen asleep. She felt as if she'd been startled awake.

Glancing toward the door now, she could see in the moonlight that there was no note. So what had awakened her? A dream? Or Rowdy singing again? She knew it could also be her visit with May Greenly that was haunting her sleep. All those things her father had sent May over the years, coming to Fortune Creek to see her. It had been true. Seth Crandell had loved the woman. Like a lot of things from her father's performances were true? She turned on the lamp beside her bed and reached for her phone. She'd wanted to get to know her father. Maybe she still could.

Many of Clay Wheaton's acts had been video recorded over the years. She found snippets, going from one to the next until she found a longer one. Sitting back against the headboard, she began to watch it hoping it was the one that mentioned May.

"What do you know about love?"

Rowdy swung his head around to look at Clay. "I'll have you know I've been in love. I had a sweetheart. Her name was May Greenly."

"I take it things didn't work out?"

Rowdy wagged his head. "We were too young, but I always keep her in my heart." Then Rowdy began to sing an old cowboy tune and she muted her phone.

She sat staring at the screen and the look on her father's face. Were all of his stories true? If so, the answer to what happened to him when he was seventeen might be in one of his performances. But she was too tired to try to find it tonight.

Molly turned off her phone and the lamp beside her bed. But as she lay back down, she doubted she was going to get any sleep. Lying there in the darkness, she heard a floorboard creak outside her room and froze, listening.

Another creak. Her eyes had adjusted to the darkness inside the room. A shaft of moonlight ran across the floor toward the door. In its ambient light, she saw her doorknob jiggle as if someone was trying to open it.

She'd never thought of herself as a screamer until the knob rattled louder and she heard the floor on the other side creak loudly as if the intruder was getting ready to bust down the door.

Chapter Fifteen

Molly blinked in the bright overhead light that chased away the shadows in her room. Ash had responded to her screams, then Georgia, then the sheriff, who'd left her and Georgia while he and Ash searched the hotel.

"Did you find him?" Molly asked when the sheriff returned.

He shook his head. "Someone went down the fire escape. It's possible they came up that way, but if so, they would have had to be let in. Unless they'd blocked the door open earlier. Ash is checking into it."

She shuddered at the thought that someone inside the hotel had helped the man get in. "Didn't I hear that the killer left a book in the door to keep it from locking on the night my father was killed?"

"So whoever tried to get into her room tonight could come back any time he wanted?" Georgia asked. "Even tonight?"

The sheriff shook his head. "He won't be coming back tonight. I'm leaving Deputy Montgomery on this floor until morning. You're safe."

"The deputy?" Georgia asked, trying to hide her smile as she rose to return to her room. "I should get back to bed."

"I'll also be staying around," Brandt added. "To make sure there are no more disturbances tonight."

Georgia looked a little crestfallen as she left, mugging a face at Molly as she went out.

After she was gone, the sheriff turned to her. "Tell me exactly what you heard."

She walked him through it feeling a little silly. "Maybe I overreacted. He just jiggled my doorknob, then a little harder and then I heard him shift on his feet as if he was going to try to knock the door down."

"You didn't overreact," he assured her. "What makes you think it was a man?"

"His boots, his step was heavy—he sounded fairly heavy."

"Whoever it was knows which room you're staying in."

"Just like the person who left the ransom note," she said suddenly, feeling wide awake again. "It could have been the same person. But how did he know my room number?"

"I'll be checking into that. In the meantime, maybe you should move to another room."

Molly shook her head. "No, we need the person with the ransom demand to come back so we can catch him."

"Yeah," the sheriff said. "We can do that without you being in this room, but we'll discuss it in the morning." He moved to her door. "You're safe. Try to get some sleep."

She looked at him as if he was delusional. "You think I can sleep after all of this?"

He smiled. "Try. I won't be far away. I'm staying in a room down the hall."

"As if that would help me sleep," she muttered under her breath. Just the thought of him nearby made her pull the blanket she was wrapped in around her. This time when she shivered it had nothing to do with the Montana cold night or her would-be intruder.

BRANDT WOKE FEELING DISORIENTED. He sat up and looked around. For a moment he didn't know where he was or what had awakened him. He'd slept fitfully after being called to the hotel last night. Even after he was sure the intruder was no longer in the hotel, he'd stayed in the lounge on the fourth floor before falling asleep and finally going to the room Ash had given him down the hall.

But once in the room, he'd kept seeing images of Molly wrapped in a blanket, her hair loose and wild, her face soft from sleep, her face flushed, her eyes shiny with fear. That alone had kept him awake for hours.

His cell phone rang, jarring him the rest of the way awake as he reached for it. "Sheriff Parker."

"I'm sorry, did I wake you?"

"Lucy," he said into the phone as he glanced at the time. Normally he would have been up and already finished with his first cup of coffee.

"Late night, but I'm up." He felt a shot of energy at just the thought that Bud Harper's sister had found something about Seth Crandell and his past that might help solve his murder.

"I've been going through old photos I told you about," she said. "I found several of Seth. He was definitely camera shy or Bud wasn't much of a photographer back then," she said. "I'm sending you the first photo."

He waited. His phone beeped. He opened the attachment. "What am I looking at?" he had to ask as he stared at a photo of a group of teens gathered in what appeared to be someone's backyard.

"Look at the two people deep in conversation on the top far left of the shot," she said. "The young male is Seth Crandell. You can't really see the young woman because she is out of the frame, but you can see part of her red dress. I'm sending another photo."

His phone beeped again. The young male had his back to the camera now, facing the young woman in the red dress. From the woman's expression the two seemed to be having an argument.

"One more," Lucy said.

He opened the next attachment. The young man had turned, was stepping out of the photo, his arm outstretched. He had hold of someone's arm, the young woman's. Part of her red dress was still in the photo—along with her upper arm.

Brandt made the photo larger until he could see the grip the man had on the woman's arm. His fingers appeared to be digging into her flesh. An uncomfortable feeling settled in his stomach. It wasn't conclusive evidence, but it was disturbing enough to make it questionable.

"Who is the young woman?" he asked, hoping Lucy would know. She did.

"Ruby Sherman." The young woman who'd died in the car crash her senior year of high school.

His mouth went dry. "Seth and Ruby?"

"Personally, I can't imagine it, but in the photos it would definitely appear that they knew each other. Maybe more than that since they seem to be having a heated argument. His grip on her surprises me. Seth was always so shy, so nice and quiet as if he was trying hard to be invisible. I was surprised he was even at the party let alone possibly with a girl. But Ruby Sherman, the most popular girl at school? You know she died that night after her car left the road and landed in the trees. Apparently she was driving way too fast."

Brandt didn't know what to say. He kept thinking about what Irma Crandell had told Molly. *Not digging up that old bone.* "There could have been a side of Seth no one knew." Except maybe Ruby Sherman. "Was there drinking at this party where the photographs were taken?"

"It was behind our house so there wasn't supposed to be, but you know how teenagers are. Someone could have sneaked in alcohol."

"You're sure this was the night she died?" he asked, his heart pounding.

"There's no date on the photos since this was before cell phones, but I remember the party and the cops showing up asking questions the next morning. Ruby's brothers swore that she would never have been driving that reckless unless someone was chasing her. To this day, they have believed someone was responsible for her so-called accident. My brother believed it too."

"You think it was Seth?"

She seemed at a loss for words for a moment. "He was always so sweet to me, the little sister who was underfoot all the time. I would have said the man couldn't have hurt a fly."

"Lucy, thank you so much for doing this. Could you please hang on to the photos? I might need them."

"There's something else." She sounded hesitant to bring it up. "Bud and Seth had a falling out before Seth left town. I never knew what it was about, but it wasn't long after Ruby died. Then Seth left and his brother Ty committed suicide. I've never put the three together before, but Ty Crandell was at the party that night. I found a photo Bud took of him. Ty was watching the party from the treehouse Bud and Seth built in our backyard. He must have been about fourteen at the time."

As Brandt disconnected, he had no idea what to do with this information. He quickly searched the *Tobacco Valley News* for the story of Ruby Sherman's accident. She'd died in late October. She'd been driving that night alone at a high rate of speed, missed a corner, the vehicle going airborne before crashing into the pines. She died at the scene. Alcohol wasn't involved, according to the coroner's report.

Ruby was the only daughter of Barnard and Nancy Sherman, owners of a company that mined gold and sapphires. The Shermans also owned a variety of local businesses, making them the leading employer in the valley. Her funeral was the largest in local history at that time.

Brandt had heard about her death growing up, a cautionary tale when it came to driving at night on these mountain roads. Also there were stories of people seeing her ghost on the spot where her car had left the road.

What her death could have to do with Clay Wheaton, he couldn't imagine. Yet he also couldn't shake the feeling that it was important to his investigation. But how it might lead him to the person who killed Clay Wheaton and took Rowdy was anyone's guess.

Chapter Sixteen

Molly could tell that the sheriff had a lot on his
mind this morning. She'd been up, showered and
dressed by the time he tapped on her door.

"Hungry?"

"Always."

"Thought we'd walk over to the café together."

"That sounds ominous," she said and laughed
as she grabbed her jacket. He didn't even smile
as she followed him down the hall.

"Mind if we take the stairs?" she asked.

He turned to look at her, frowning. "If this is
about getting your steps in—"

"It's about not riding in that elevator," she
said heading down the stairs. The moment she
cleared the lobby and pushed out into the street,
she turned to the sheriff. "So what's going on?"

"I just thought you might want breakfast," he
said defensively.

She eyed him, not buying it. "I don't want to
move out of my room."

"Fine." He started walking toward the café.

She had to run to catch up. "I'm not leaving town either."

"Whatever you say." He didn't even bother to look at her when he said it.

"I'm staying here until my father's killer is caught."

He stopped and spun around to face her, so abruptly she almost collided with him. "What? This isn't about Rowdy anymore? I thought that was the only reason you were here."

She glared at him, hands going to her hips. "You found out something you don't want to tell me." His mouth snapped shut as if he was shocked that she knew him so well. She was even more shocked that she'd been right. "You might as well go ahead and tell me and not ruin my breakfast with this mood you're in."

"Has anyone ever told you what an exasperating, infuriating, maddening woman you are?"

"Someone might have mentioned that before. Your point?"

He sighed, dragged off his Stetson and raked a hand through his thick sandy-blond hair before he settled those blue eyes on her again. "I hate how involved you've become in this murder investigation. It's put you in danger already and the more I learn, the more I wish you'd put your shapely behind on a plane back to New York City."

SHE SMILED, looking up at him with those big, luminous Montana-sky-blue eyes. "You think my backside is shapely?"

He groaned. "That's your takeaway?"

"No, I heard you say I was right. You found out something you don't want to tell me about." That smug look said she knew him too well. The worst part was that she did. How had this happened? He'd barely known this woman a matter of days and now he couldn't imagine a day without her around.

He stood in the street looking at her for a few moments before he shook his head and turned toward the café. "Breakfast first." He'd slowed down where she didn't have any trouble keeping up, studying her out of the corner of his eye and reminding himself that once the investigation was over, she'd be gone. She'd be putting that shapely backside on the next plane. That did nothing to improve his mood.

It was a beautiful spring day, the air crisp and clear scented with pine and falling dried aspen leaves. He led Molly out on the patio along the side of the café so they could have some privacy. "You going to be warm enough out here?" he asked. She nodded and took a seat. He watched her look toward the mountains before turning her gaze on him again.

He thought about apologizing for what he'd said about her, but had a feeling she'd heard worse. She was the kind of woman men would try to put a rope on, thinking they could tame that headstrong stubbornness out of her. But breaking Molly to his will was the last thing he wanted to do.

"I spoke with Lucy Gunther," he said after Alice had taken their orders and gone back inside. They were alone, no one within earshot.

"The sister of the man who was my father's friend," she said.

"She remembered Seth as a sweet, shy, nice friend of her brother's. That's about all she could tell me, but she said her brother took a lot of photos growing up and that she'd gone through them." Molly leaned forward, all her attention on him, the intent glow in her eyes stronger than the sunlight shining on them through the trees.

He cleared his throat. "She found some photos of Seth and a girl. They appeared to be arguing."

"That's it?" Molly said. "You think this is the girl he got in trouble with?"

"Maybe. The thing is, the girl, Ruby Sherman, was the one you found the story on, the one who was killed in an automobile accident the night the photos were taken of your father and Ruby."

"Am I missing something?"

"Her parents have both passed since then, but she has two older brothers, Tom and Alex. Whenever their sister's name comes up, both brothers claim she had to have been chased that night by another vehicle that forced her off the road. It was never proved. As far as I know there was no evidence to substantiate this claim. But she's kind of become a folk heroine. There's a shrine out on the highway where her car went off the road." He looked away. "There have been people who swear they've seen her ghost. Legend has it she can't rest until—"

"Her killer is brought to justice," Molly finished for him. "You think my father might have chased her that night?"

He shrugged. "Truthfully, I don't know what to think. When your grandmother told you that Seth had to leave because of some young woman, I figured maybe he'd gotten a girl in town pregnant, something like that. I never imagined it might have something to do with Ruby Sherman, let alone possibly her death."

Alice brought out their breakfasts and retreated back inside the café. Molly picked up her fork, but didn't begin to eat even though her stomach was growling. "Is it possible he was responsible for her losing control and crashing into the trees? If so, he killed that girl and he never came forward. But why?"

"Also, why would he have been forced to join the military unless…"

Molly nodded. "Unless his father found out what he'd done."

Chapter Seventeen

Molly thought that she wouldn't be able to eat a bite after the sheriff had told her his news. But hunger won out and while she barely tasted the food, she dug in as she tried to process what he'd told her. "So he could have chased her, not realizing how dangerous it was or how tragically it would end," she said between bites. "I guess I can see that happening and if he was this sensitive guy Lucy thought he was, he would have been traumatized. So why not come forward that night? Don't you feel like there is more to the story?"

The sheriff nodded as he ate.

"I wonder, if they were arguing at the party, what it was about," she said thinking out loud. "You don't chase someone you barely know, right? If he did chase her." Molly wasn't expecting an answer and didn't wait for one. "It just doesn't sound like the man everyone thought my father was."

"His brother Ty was also at that party that night," the sheriff said lifting a fork. "What that might have to do with anything I have no idea. But Ty committed suicide after Seth left the ranch."

"I wish we knew more about the family dynamic between Seth and his family especially his brother Ty," she said. "Maybe if they were close and Seth's leaving pushed him to take his life..." Molly looked up at the sheriff. "You're thinking Ruby fits into this puzzle, aren't you." He looked as if he was about to warn her not to be telling him what he was thinking.

"Don't bother denying it, Sheriff," she said with a shake of her head. "I'm thinking the same thing. How did Ty get to the party? I guess he could have come with friends."

"He wasn't with friends at the party."

"So if Seth left right after Ruby, how did Ty get home? He wasn't driving, not at... How old was he?"

"Fourteen."

She finished her breakfast and pushed her plate away. When she looked up, he had finished eating, had leaned back and was now studying her openly. *"What?"*

"Since you seem to know me so well, maybe you can call me something besides sheriff. My name's Brandt."

She smiled, but she wasn't sure that was a good idea. Thinking of him as sheriff seemed to put an invisible barrier between them. The memory of yesterday in her hotel room was still fresh. If either of them had even blinked they could have been lip-locked. Then there was last night in her hotel room. She didn't doubt that one kiss would have led to another and with the hotel bed right there in the room...

"Brandt," she said trying out his name on her lips and saw him staring at those lips. His look sent a fissure of heat to her center. "Yeah, maybe I'll stick to sheriff."

BRANDT SWORE TO himself as Alice came out to clear their dishes. He saw her curious look as she glanced at him, then Molly, then him again. Unfortunately, the entire town—who was he kidding—the entire county probably knew about his last disastrous love affair. Not that he and Molly were headed for a love affair.

But it was clear that some people in town were worried that he was headed down that precariously rutted road again. He dragged his gaze from her to look out the window and felt a start as he saw Ash Hammond coming down the street with Tom Sherman. Brandt couldn't remember the last time he'd seen Tom in Fortune Creek.

The two men stopped at a dark-colored SUV, talking animatedly.

"Now what?" Molly asked as she glanced in the direction he had been looking.

"Ash and Tom. I forgot they're cousins," Brandt said more to himself than to Molly. "They used to be close in high school. Played football together in high school. Haven't seen Tom around Fortune Creek for a while though."

"Is it my imagination or is everyone in this county related?"

Brandt chuckled. "Seems like it. Have to be careful what you say about just about anyone in Montana, especially in these small towns. As large as the state is, you'd be surprised how many people are related. It makes Montana a lot smaller. Alice is second or third cousin with May Greenly. Cora if I'm not mistaken is a distant cousin of the Crandells and half the county since her maiden name was Olson. Roots run deep here."

"But not for you?"

He shrugged. "We moved here when my father took the sheriff job. All my relatives are spread across the country. I always envied my friends who had more cousins than you could shake a stick at."

"Shake a stick at?"

"Sorry, my grandmother. She had a lot of sayings and some of them kind of stuck."

Molly looked to the street in time to see Tom's car window power down, Ash still talking to him in the middle of the street for a few moments before Tom Sherman drove away. She frowned. "Tom and Ash are first cousins?"

"Tom's dad was a Sherman, his mother a Hammond, like Alice and May Greenly, first cousins,

I think, might be second or third. Hard to keep track."

She gave him an impatient look. "All these cousins who can just come and go in Fortune Creek with no one thinking anything about it? If Tom and his family suspected Ruby's accident wasn't an accident like you said and he found out about Seth and Ruby…and Clay Wheaton…"

He chuckled. "I know where you're headed with this," Brandt said. "I'm already there. Tom had access to the hotel. Shall we go?" At her nod, he tossed down his napkin, rose from his chair and reached for his Stetson. He was already thinking about what he would say to Ash when they reached the hotel. He warned himself to be diplomatic. Tom Sherman was Ash's blood. Not that blood could save you when it came to murder.

Chapter Eighteen

The sheriff had a steely look in his eye as they walked up the street to the hotel. Molly could feel the determination coming off him. She hadn't realized how hard his job was here in this small town. He knew everyone, had spent a lot of his life in this town with these people. How hard it must be to have to arrest one of them, to put his feelings aside, to do his duty.

She wanted to touch one of those broad shoulders, to offer sympathy, but she knew it wasn't what he needed right now. So she kept her mouth shut and simply walked through the beautiful morning on this mountain. The air was so pure up here, the scents so filled with pine and aspen and earthy smells, she didn't recognize it as air. She'd grown up in the city smelling exhaust.

At the hotel entrance, the sheriff opened the door for her, ushering her in. She headed for the stairs as behind her, she heard the sheriff say, "Ash, need to ask you a few questions" in his authoritative lawman voice.

She was thinking about how their conversation might go, when she realized that she hadn't seen Georgia this morning. She climbed the stairs, taking her time. She kept thinking about earlier in the café with Brandt—the sheriff—she quickly corrected. Best keep that silver star between them.

Molly knocked at Georgia's door, but there was no answer. That seemed strange. There weren't that many places to go in Fortune Creek. Maybe she'd taken off with that deputy she seemed to have a crush on. If so, Molly envied her. It would be freeing to just let go and take what she wanted.

The thought startled her as she reached for the key to her room. The huge key fob weighed a ton and always fell to the bottom of her purse. Take what she wanted? Where had that thought come from followed on its heels by the image of Brandt lounging on her hotel room bed?

Groaning to herself, she opened her hotel room door. Her bed was made, no half-naked sheriff on it. Instead, there was a folded sheet of hotel stationery lying on the floor just inside the door in a shaft of sunlight.

Her pulse jumped at the sight before she closed the door and reached for her phone.

Chapter Nineteen

"What are you trying to say?" Ash demanded. "You can't possibly think that Tom had anything to do with this."

"Don't make this any harder than it is. Did you see him the day Clay Wheaton was murdered?"

"No." He shook his head but even as he did, he frowned. "I…" Ash swallowed. "Maybe I did." The new hotel proprietor looked miserable.

"He was in the hotel that day? What time?"

"Afternoon." Ash looked sick. "He would have no reason to kill anyone let alone some old ventriloquist who was staying here."

"He might have a reason," the sheriff said. "Did he go upstairs?"

Ash sighed and nodded. "He asked about the remodeling project and if it was all right if he ran up to check it out. I'd gotten busy with a guest and told him to go on up."

"Did you talk to him again when he came back down?"

"I…" He shook his head. "I was busy. He was

in a hurry. He just waved on his way through the lobby."

"Did he seem upset?"

"I don't know." He swore. "Tom wouldn't—"

Brandt's phone rang. He saw it was Molly and excused himself to take it. He had begun to worry that they weren't going to hear from Rowdy's alleged kidnapper again so was glad to hear there was another ransom note. "I'll be right up. Don't—"

"I know," she said. "I'll be waiting out in the hall for you."

He disconnected and looked at Ash who appeared sick. "Please don't mention this to Tom."

"I just don't understand why you'd even think—"

"I can't explain right now. Just keep it between the two of us." Ash nodded and Brandt hurried upstairs, hoping Molly had done as he'd asked. He found her standing in the hallway, just as she said she would be.

"Did you read it?" he asked when she unlocked the door.

"No, you told me not to touch it." She stood back to let him enter first.

"Yeah, but you hardly ever do what I tell you to," he said over his shoulder as she followed him inside. "You don't follow orders all that well."

"I don't like taking orders." He could see how much all of this was weighing her down. He wished there was some way he could help her other than to find out the truth about her father—and find the murderer.

"I've noticed." The problem was that he wasn't sure finding Clay Wheaton's killer would help her though. It took all of his strength not to step to her, put his arms around her and try to ease her pain. But he couldn't cross that line, especially now when she'd just poured her heart out to him. She was confused, looking for a reassurance he couldn't give her.

He pulled out the gloves and unfolded one of the evidence bags he always carried. After pulling on the gloves, he finally reached down and picked up the folded sheet of hotel stationery.

"WHAT DOES IT SAY?" Molly asked as he unfolded it. She moved closer to read over his shoulder. Like last time, the note was written on Fortune Creek Hotel stationery. Only this time, the alleged kidnapper hadn't used the leaky pen. This time it was also more threatening toward Rowdy.

"It gives us a different place to drop off the money," he told her.

"I saw," she said as she stepped back. The sheriff smelled really good today. Standing that close to him earlier, she'd taken in the male scent of him, breathing a little too deeply. It wasn't good being this aware of the man. "The person is threatening to destroy Rowdy unless the money is left at the drop site. So what are we going to do?" she asked. "I don't have the money yet."

"We're not going to hand over five thousand dollars. What we're going to do is find out if the person has Rowdy. Then arrest him or her either for extortion or murder or both. You might remember I'm trying to catch a murderer?"

"I'm aware of that. But I thought we were going to try to get Rowdy back—and catch the killer when the person picked up the money."

The sheriff studied the note again. "This appears to be an inexperienced kidnapper. He should have given us a phone number so we could talk to him and make arrangements. Instead he expects us to drop off thousands of dollars in the woods? He's kidding himself."

"So we do nothing again?"

"I dropped off a note at the last drop site demanding proof that he had Rowdy. The person either didn't check the site or doesn't have Rowdy. Clearly, he's inexperienced at this, but he's not fool enough to just quit if he has the puppet. He probably isn't the killer." He finally looked at her. "Are you okay?"

"I'm okay," she said and sat down on the bed. "It's just all of this." She sighed. "I keep wondering. Who would my father open his door to knowing that they had come to kill him?"

"We don't know that was the case."

"Don't we? We know he came back here to say

goodbye because he had unfinished business. It might have something to do with Ruby's death or his brother Ty's suicide or something else entirely. My father came here knowing he was already drying. He wasn't afraid of whoever he opened that door to the night he died or he wouldn't have come back here."

The sheriff raked a hand through his hair. "Wait, you think your father came here to say goodbye?"

She met his gaze. "I guess I didn't mention it. I doubted it would interest you."

He groaned as he got the chair from the corner, dragged it over and sat down in front of her. "You'd be surprised at what I'm interested in." His impatient look seemed to ask if he was going to have to pull the words out of her.

"He and May Greenly were in love when they were young," she said finally. "Did you know that? Apparently, he never got over her. She says she doesn't know why he left at seventeen, why he changed his name, why he did everything that he did. But he did go see her when he got to Fortune Creek. He went to tell her goodbye."

Brandt seemed to process all that for a moment. "So that's what he said he was doing in Fortune Creek."

"Not entirely. She said he had unfinished business to take care of."

"She didn't know what?"

Molly shook her head. "I'm learning things about my father that I never knew. I listened to one of his shows online where Rowdy said that May Greenly was his true love. I suspect now that all the stories he told through Rowdy were based on some truth. Everything I needed to know about him was there had I paid attention. I didn't think anything about his act was real."

"I wonder if what happened to force him to leave and change his name is also somewhere in those stories in his act," Brandt said thoughtfully.

"I thought of that too," she said, though she doubted the name of the killer was there. "I'm just afraid there is something much darker, much worse to find out. What if he followed Ruby, forced her off the road that night? What if he could have saved her but didn't?"

"We don't know she was the young woman your grandmother mentioned. But I feel as if it is getting more dangerous for you to be here. You know you don't have to stay in Fortune Creek. In fact, I really wish you would go back to New York."

She narrowed her eyes at him. "You've made that perfectly clear. I'm not going anywhere."

"What about your job?"

"It'll be there or it won't. At this point I'm not sure I care. I think I became a financial analyst because of my father. I wanted a career that was real. Numbers don't lie. I didn't want to be my father. I wanted something solid under my feet that

I could count on. Now… I'm not sure it's what I want to do with the rest of my life."

"I wouldn't make any hasty decisions about your future if I was you. All of this has come as a shock. Give yourself some time and I'm sure you'll be winging your way back to New York City and your life there."

She met his gaze then, measuring his words. "Maybe." Rising, she then walked to the window and looked out. She turned from there to look at him. "Are you going to leave another note at the new drop site?"

"That would be sheriff's department business."

Molly was looking at him as if she could read his mind. "You're planning to set up some kind of trap for him, aren't you?" She didn't give him a chance to answer which was just as well since he didn't plan on telling her anyway. "I'm going with you."

"No, you aren't," he said as he rose from the chair and put it back where he found it.

"I have to," she said. "I'm the one who should leave the note. If you're spotted, you'll scare the person off."

"This is Fortune Creek. Even if not related, everyone knows everybody's business. The kidnapper knows that you told me about the note—trust me. There're no secrets here."

"I'm not so sure about that. My father had secrets and so far we haven't been able to dig them all up. I think there's more going on than you think. You didn't even know about May Greenly."

He sighed. "I know you went to visit her."

"Oh, yeah?" she challenged. "Did you know about her and my father? Did you know that he sent her little treasures from every place he performed? Did you know that they were in love, that their parents wouldn't let them marry?"

"I knew that she had a boyfriend years ago. Someone who broke her heart and that's why she's never married. If you're suggesting that she killed him..."

"Of course not. That's why she's always stayed here as if she thought he would come back. He did come back. To die. To pay for some past sin. To tell her that he loved her, and she told him that she loved him. It's a tragic love story and I'm part of it now, which is why I'm the one who's getting the ransom notes."

Brandt groaned inwardly. This woman was so independent, so determined, so dangerous. Those blue eyes of hers met his. He saw her fiery spirit, all that defiance burning bright. He actually liked that about her. Except for the part where she was going to make his job much harder—and he feared get herself killed.

"You can hide in the woods or whatever it is you do to set your trap," she said, rushing on before he could speak. "You just let me know where to pick you up."

Right now he wished he wasn't the sheriff. He wished he was just some cowboy standing in a pretty, young woman's bedroom wishing to hell he had her on that bed. "You're going to make me regret this, aren't you?" he asked.

She took a step toward him. "It depends on what you're thinking you're going to regret," she said.

He had to smile because damned if he wasn't positive that she really could read his mind. He saw her eyes shift to the bed and then up at him. Not an invitation—not exactly. But apparently, they were at least at the same rodeo.

Brandt had never wanted an investigation to be over as much as he did this one. This woman was like none he'd ever met. He told himself she'd be the death of him if he wasn't careful. He wished that wasn't so close to the truth. He had to keep his wits about him, reminding himself he was on the trail of a murderer. And he felt he was getting close.

Which meant he had to keep Molly at arm's length—at least until the investigation was over. That was if she ended up staying that long. She swore she was seeing it through to the very end. It would be like her to do just that and get herself killed.

He couldn't let that happen. How he was going

to stop her was another thing. The worst part was that he knew what would happen once the investigation was over. After she had Rowdy and put her father to rest, she would go back to her life. She'd be gone before he could say lickety-split. Fortune Creek was no place for a woman like her. This woman couldn't be corralled like some wild horse. He told himself he was too smart to even try.

"Okay," he said, clearly surprising her. She'd been winding up for a battle and now he laid down his weapons and surrendered.

She was staring at him as if not quite believing it as he picked up the bagged note. "You aren't just trying to mollify me, right?"

He shook his head. "Like you said, you're the one getting the notes. You should be the one to take our response to the kidnapper out in the woods in the middle of the night." Molly eyed him with suspicion, making him laugh. "I'll be going with you—not where anyone will know I'm there except you. Still, it could be dangerous. But you only live once, right?"

"You're trying to scare me."

"You should be scared," he said more firmly. "This isn't a game. There's a killer out there. Remember last night the person outside your hotel room?" He saw her swallow. "Right. He could be the person you're so willing to meet in the woods alone in the dark."

"If you're trying to talk me out of it—"

"No, because you're right about him wanting you to deliver the money late tonight. I just want you to know that this might not be about Rowdy at all. It could be about you, the ventriloquist's daughter, and the killer wanting to finish what he started."

Chapter Twenty

Irma Crandell parked the old pickup in the trees at the edge of town where she had a view of the hotel. She saw in the soft earth that she wasn't the first person to park here recently. She thought of her husband. Or maybe Gage. Or maybe one of his sons.

She couldn't worry about that right now as she considered what she'd done—taking a ranch truck for a second time and leaving without telling Cecil or anyone else. It seemed a minor thing, especially considering what she was about to do. Last night she'd heard Cecil get up in the middle of the night and leave the ranch in his truck. That was when she'd known she couldn't wait any longer.

She hated herself for not taking things into her own hands years ago. Her precious son had been lost to her and now he was dead. She had no doubt that Cecil had killed him rather than let him return to the ranch and her. She would deal with Cecil later. It was Seth's daughter she'd come to see.

She'd sat in this same spot yesterday. This morning she'd seen the young woman leave with the sheriff to walk down the street to the café. Interesting how close the two walked together. Maybe too close. They'd both gone into the hotel. Finally, the sheriff emerged. No sign of the girl. What Irma was waiting for was the hotel owner. Yesterday he'd come out at one o'clock on the nose, walked over to the convenience store. He'd eaten his lunch on the bench out front and when his hour was up, he'd walked back to the hotel.

Today a friend had joined him, and Irma had worried that he might change his routine. But when he and the friend came out and headed for the convenience store, she knew it was her chance.

She popped open the pickup door and headed for the hotel. Just as she'd hoped, the lobby was empty. It didn't take her long to figure out what room Molly was in. Only two keys were missing from rooms on the fourth floor. She took the stairs even though it was slow going up the flights.

Once she came out on the top floor, she took a moment to catch her breath and make sure she still had the knife in her pocket. Cecil had handguns, but most of them he kept locked up and she didn't have a key. She wasn't about to come to town totin' his old shotgun.

She knocked at the first door she came to, tapping lightly with her free hand. The other hand gripped the handle of the knife.

Chapter Twenty-One

After leaving Molly, Brandt drove into Eureka. He found Tom Sherman behind a large desk in the office of one of his deceased father's businesses. He looked the part in chinos and a button-down shirt, his blazer tossed over a nearby chair.

"I can give you a few minutes," Tom said offering him an empty chair. "I have a meeting."

"I need to ask you about the night Ruby was killed."

Tom blinked, his face going stony. "Too bad the law didn't care all those years ago."

"You've been pretty vocal in the past about what you think happened. As I recall, you suspected Seth Crandell was responsible. I need to know what that suspicion was based on. I'm sure you remember that night."

Tom sat forward in his chair, forearms on his desk. "I wish I didn't remember. Ruby had just turned seventeen. Dad let her go to a party at the Harpers' house. Alex was fourteen and got to go to a sleepover. I was eight and mad that I had to stay home. I just remember waking up to cop cars in front of the house, my mother hysterical, my father furious and demanding answers."

"Did he get answers?"

"Over the next few days it became pretty clear. Alex and I had overheard Ruby complaining about this Crandell boy following her around, refusing to leave her alone. Dad said he would handle it, but he didn't get around to it. Then when we heard that Seth Crandell had been seen at the party with Ruby and they'd been arguing... Seth had left right after she did and seemed in a hurry." He sat forward, his gaze intent. "He chased her. It is the only thing that makes sense. She would have never driven that fast unless she was afraid and trying to get back to the ranch and safety."

"That is one theory," Brandt said.

Tom sat back, his face flushing with anger. "It wasn't just a theory. Your dad dragged his feet on arresting Seth and the next thing we knew he'd gone into the military to escape punishment."

"Had there been any solid evidence—"

"*Solid evidence?* Everyone knew what he'd done. He was responsible for killing my sister and destroying my family."

"Destroying your family?"

"My parents split up by the end of that year. Alex and I were forced to move to Colorado with our mother... Yeah, he destroyed our family. My mother never got over Ruby's death. I don't think my father did either. Put them both into early graves."

"Did you ever see Seth again?"

Tom looked away for a moment, his jaw working as he tried to tamp down his anger. "I tried to find him when I got older. No luck."

"What would you have done if you had found him?"

His gaze came back to Brandt. After a moment, he shrugged. "Beat him up."

"Kill him?"

Tom scoffed and got to his feet. "Thanks for this trip down memory lane, but I really need to get going or I'll miss my appointment."

The sheriff rose as well, waiting for Tom to ask why he was looking into Ruby's death after all these years. Or why he was asking questions about Seth Crandell. He didn't inquire as Brandt left.

MOLLY WAS ON the phone with her boss when she heard the soft tap at her door. She assumed it was Georgia who she hadn't seen all morning. She hoped the woman hadn't taken it on herself to meet with the people who claimed to have Rowdy.

"Take all the time you need," her boss was saying on the other end of the call. "Your father dying... You've had a shock." He had no idea. "Don't make any rash decisions." Same advice the sheriff had given her.

"I have to go." She disconnected and was headed

for the door when she heard another tap, this one louder. "Hold your horses. I'm coming." She threw open the door.

The smile on her face turned to shock at the sight of Irma Crandell standing in the hallway.

"We need to talk," Irma said, pushing past her and into the room, where she stopped to glance around as if she'd never seen a hotel room before. "Close the door."

Too surprised to argue, she closed the door as her mind raced. What was Irma doing here? Her grandmother had told her not to come back to the ranch. Molly had assumed that meant she would never see any of the Crandells again, especially her grandmother.

"You need to leave town," Irma said glancing toward the closet and Molly's suitcase. "It's not safe for you here."

She wondered if this woman was so used to being ordered around that she thought she could do it to the granddaughter she had pretty much denied. "I'm not going anywhere until I find out who killed my father."

Irma's dark gaze pivoted to her. "He was my son. I'll see that the killer gets what's comin' to him."

"If you know who killed my father, you need to tell the sheriff."

The older woman scoffed. "You don't know nothing about it."

Molly crossed her arms, standing her ground even as her pulse thundered a warning in her ears. "I know about Ruby Sherman." She'd thrown it out there, unsure how it would fly.

From the stricken look on Irma's face, it had hit its mark. "You don't want to be saying nothing about that."

"Tell me what happened that night," she said, aware she was taking a hell of a chance pushing this woman. "Why did he chase her?"

Irma stood stone still, one hand in the pocket of her long jacket, the other clenched at her side.

"Please," Molly said. "Help me to understand." For a moment she thought the woman would come flying at her, Irma's gaze was so deadly intense.

When she spoke, it was in a whisper. "He was just a boy." She slowly dropped down on the edge at the end of the bed. For a moment she seemed distracted by how soft the mattress was. She placed her free hand on it, her other hand buried deep in the pocket of her old coat. She finally looked up at Molly.

"He didn't know no better, followin' a girl like her around, spyin' on her, thinkin' he could... That she would... She was playin' with him, makin' him a fool behind his back like he weren't nobody." Her voice broke.

"The night of the party," Molly clarified. "According to the sheriff, there were photographs of Ruby and Seth having an argument. Also a photo that showed that Ty was there too, watching from a treehouse on the property."

"Ty." Irma's eyes filled with tears. "It weren't nothing but a crush. He were fourteen. He didn't mean no harm. You know that girl lead him on. Then she was going 'round saying things about Ty, about the family. Seth wasn't about to let that stand."

Not Seth, but Ty? She thought of the photo the sheriff had told her about. Seth arguing with Ruby. About what she'd said about his brother? "So he did follow Ruby that night?"

Irma shook her head as if irritated that Molly hadn't been listening. "Ty's the one couldn't stay away from that girl. Seth was just tryin' to save 'em both. He spotted Ty hidin' in the back of 'er car. Seth went after Ruby scared at what Ty might do. Or what that girl might do, when she seen Ty hidin' in the backseat. But he didn't catch up till… till it were too late."

The pieces finally fell into place. Seth had been arguing with Ruby over how she'd been treating his younger brother. Ty must have overheard. When Ruby left the party, Ty was hiding in the backseat of her car. Seth saw him and went after them. "Ty wasn't hurt when Ruby crashed her car?" she asked.

"Nar a scratch cuz he was in the backseat. Seth hauled him out. Ruby was gone, nothin' he could do, couldn't stick around, weren't no purpose. Ty had her blood all over him, cryin' sayin' he loved her, wanted to die with her. Seth brang him home, cleaned him up. When the law came round askin' questions, Seth lied for his brother. Cecil could tell he were lyin'." She shook her head. "Seth wouldn't tell on Ty, just kept lyin'. Cecil wanted him gone. Been comin', weren't nothin' I could do 'bout it. Should-a stopped Cecil. Should-a ended it right there."

"Seth had to know that leaving the way he did made him look guilty," Molly said. Irma had fallen silent, no doubt lost in the past. "Ty...he took his life?"

"Couple weeks later. Left a note tellin' what he'd done. I burnt it." She looked up, something behind the dampness in her eyes that gave Molly a chill. "Ty were Cecil's favorite. Let 'im live thinkin' Ty done it cuz of Cecil sendin' Seth away."

Molly felt sick at the hatred that ran so deep in that family. Her blood, she reminded herself, thinking of how she'd never been able to forgive her father for leaving her and her mother. Wasn't that why she had to see this through? She couldn't make it up to her father. But she could see his killer was caught.

She realized her father had been lucky to leave here and the Crandells. But his upbringing had scarred him. Only seventeen, he probably left blaming himself for all of it.

"Who killed my father?" she asked her grandmother.

"Told you," Irma said as she rose stiffly and closed the distance between them. "Don't mind yourself with that. Best pack up and leave while you can."

"Aren't you worried I'll tell the sheriff what you told me?"

Irma was so close Molly could smell the sour scent of cooked food on her clothes. "You go blabbin' to the sheriff..." She seemed to finger something in her coat pocket where her one hand had remained since she'd walked into the room. "Too late to brang shame on us anymore. You do what you got to do."

With that, her grandmother walked slowly to the door, her gait filled with both physical and mental pain as she stepped out, closed it behind her and was gone.

Chapter Twenty-Two

Brandt noticed that Molly still seemed to be upset as she told him about Irma's visit. "Well, that solves one mystery."

She seemed to notice his lack of surprise. "That's all you have to say?"

"Sorry, I figured it might be something like that. One son sent away, another commits suicide shortly thereafter because he is actually the guilty one. I'd looked into the old case. Didn't find anything, but the timing had bothered me because of Seth's leaving. I'd just never put it together with Ruby Sherman's car accident. Now all three are dead. Doubt Irma would come forward with her story on the record. Not that it would change the past."

"But it could be why Cecil Crandell doesn't want it to come out."

Brandt agreed. "I spoke with Tom Sherman after I left you."

"Ruby's brother?"

"He was only eight the night she died, but what

he told me fits with what Irma told you. Ruby had complained about a Crandell boy following her around. She'd just apparently not told them which one."

"So that's why they thought Seth was responsible," Molly said. "Which gives Tom and his brother a motive for murder."

"Alex isn't in the country."

"But Tom is," she said.

The sheriff nodded. "He definitely blames Seth, said after he grew up, he tried to find him. Said he might have beat him up if he had."

"What else would he admit to a sheriff?" She seemed to see his hesitancy. "You think he's capable of murder?"

"I think everyone is capable under certain circumstances." He didn't mention that he was tracking down anyone in the area who had a legal permit for a gun suppressor—or as they called them on television, a silencer. As for illegal suppressors, he didn't even venture to guess how many there might be.

"What?" Molly asked as if seeing him fighting what he needed to say.

Damn. It seemed she could read him like yesterday's newspaper. "I think Irma was right. You should go home."

She gave him a sideways look as those blue eyes fired with impatience.

"You're not safe here. I wrote a note asking for

a photo of today's paper and Rowdy. I dropped it off at the second ransom demand spot. If the alleged kidnapper finds it before tonight…"

"He'll either come with a photo of Rowdy or not show up at all," Molly said. "If this person has Rowdy…" Her voice broke. "Then he's the killer."

"Not necessarily," he said, but she wasn't listening.

"Don't try to stop me. I talked to my boss today. He tried to talk me out of it, but I have to see this through even if it means quitting my job."

"Molly—"

"I can't leave." Her voice broke. "I owe it to my father who I'm only now getting to know. He tried to reach me through Rowdy. I wasn't listening. I'm listening now. I was going through his old performances when Irma stopped by. But now I wonder if we don't already know who killed my father. We just need to catch him at the drop site tonight."

Brandt was momentarily at a loss for words. "This is all my fault. I shouldn't have involved you in this investigation." He saw her expression and quickly added, "You *did* help. A lot. But I can't let you risk your life. The murderer has already killed once. I suspect it will come easier the next time."

They both started at the sound of a knock at her door. They exchanged a look and Molly rose to answer it as Brandt stepped out of sight.

"WE NEED TO TALK," Georgia said the moment Molly opened the door and the insurance agent rushed in on a cool burst of spring air. Her face was flushed, her eyes bright.

"You found Rowdy?" the sheriff asked.

Georgia looked surprised to see him there and confused for a moment. "No."

Molly was in no mood to play games after her talk with the sheriff. He was trying to scare her. She didn't need him to tell her that she was out of her lane. Her life had been carefully planned and executed—until now.

But that didn't change how she felt. She wasn't going anywhere—except to the spot where the ransom note had told her to go tonight.

She turned her attention to Georgia, ignoring the lawman. "Then what are you so excited about?" she demanded.

"The deputy," Georgia whispered as if this hadn't gone as well as she'd thought it would. "He asked me out."

"So you haven't heard back from any of the people who'd contacted you about the reward?" Molly asked.

Georgia shook her head and glanced toward the sheriff as he made his way toward the door. Clearly, she hated that the sheriff had been right.

"I will leave you…ladies to your…celebration." His gaze moved to Molly. "Remember what I said." She mugged a face at him as he left.

"What was that about?" Georgia asked.

"Nothing," Molly said, waving it off. "So you and the deputy?"

Her new friend beamed; her excitement, while dimmed earlier, was now back. "I can't remember the last time I had a real date where I didn't have to swipe right or go Dutch. But I need something to wear."

"Don't look at me," Molly said. "I brought a minimum change of clothes thinking this trip wouldn't take long."

"Can we go into town shopping? Please. I want to buy something special."

"You'll look good in anything you wear," Molly tried to reassure her. But she could see that Georgia wanted a new outfit to wear on this date tonight. She glanced at the time. She still had plenty of it before the ransom note drop. "Fine, let me grab the keys to the rental." She stepped away, thinking a shopping trip was exactly what she needed after Irma's visit and then the sheriff's. Actually, she might buy a black outfit to wear tonight since she would probably be hiding in the woods. "Let's go," she said to Georgia. "What time is your date?"

"Six."

They had plenty of time. "Is there any place in Eureka to shop?"

"I looked online. There are several places."

Molly couldn't help smiling as they climbed

into the rental car and headed for what they now thought of as the big city. "You and the deputy? Is it…serious?" she asked as she drove.

"It's just a date."

"And you're just excited because you haven't been on one for a while."

Georgia laughed. "Jaden is a hunk but after Rowdy is found, I'll be on a plane home."

"Are you telling me that this is just a wild fling?"

"Haven't you thought about having a fling with the sheriff?"

Molly smiled. "Whatever happens in Montana, stays in Montana?"

"Exactly." Georgia's phone rang. She checked it and didn't take the call, but she looked upset.

"Was that the insurance company calling about Rowdy?" Molly had to ask.

Her friend shook her head. "Just…an old boyfriend." She turned on the radio and began to sing along to the country station as they drove toward Eureka.

An hour later, Molly's feet hurt. She found a bench just outside the last store she and Georgia had visited. Finding the perfect dress had turned out to be quite an ordeal. Fortunately, she'd found one inside this store since it was the last one in town. The dress had been beautiful on her, Molly thought smiling to herself.

She realized that she hadn't felt like that about a

date since... She laughed to herself. She couldn't remember if she'd ever felt giddy over a man. She thought of the sheriff. A few plucked heartstrings and several slightly indecent thoughts didn't count.

Georgia came out of the store beaming just as the clerk put out the closed sign. "We have to hurry," she said sounding breathless as she checked the time. The day had cooled.

"Don't worry, I'll get you back in plenty of time." Molly rose from the bench laughing as they started to cross the street.

A truck came flying around the corner pulling a horse trailer. Molly jumped back, dragging Georgia with her. She was about to shout at the driver when the driver threw on the brakes and jumped out. The passenger side of the truck flew open. At first she thought both were coming to apologize and see if she and Georgia were all right, when she got a good look at what appeared to be two people wearing rubber Halloween masks that covered their entire heads.

The larger of the two grabbed Georgia. Before Molly could react, the other one grabbed her, wrenching her purse away as they half dragged her to the open stock trailer door and shoved her inside. She fell to the trailer floor, Georgia joining her as the door was slammed shut. As Molly stumbled to her feet, the truck engine roared and the trailer began to move, knocking her to her knees.

"What is going on?" Georgia demanded.

Molly didn't know for sure, but she feared it had something to do with her father's murder and his missing dummy. She moved over next to Georgia as the truck and stock trailer sped out of town. "Do you have your phone?" She had to raise her voice over the rattle of the trailer and roar of the truck engine.

Georgia shook her head, looking as if she was in shock. "He took my purse." She was clutching the bag with her new dress inside to her chest as if it was a life raft and they were at sea and sinking. "Who... What..." She burst into tears. "This is not what I was hoping for when I came to Montana. I'm going to be late for my date and I can't even make a call."

Molly wanted to reassure her, but from what she could see of the landscape flying by through the gaps in the side of the metal trailer, they weren't headed for Fortune Creek. They were headed away from Eureka and into the wild country outside town.

Molly looked around the stock trailer. Even if she could unlock the door and open it, the truck was going too fast to jump out. Nor did she think she could talk Georgia into leaping out onto the highway as dark pines rushed past.

But she had to do something. While she had no idea who these kidnappers were or what they had planned, she wasn't naive enough to hope that she and Georgia weren't in trouble. Worse, she feared it had something to do with her and her father's death. Was it possible one of them had killed her father? What if they had Rowdy and there was no doubt at least one of them was capable of murder?

Not that it mattered at this point. There was nothing in the trailer to use for a weapon let alone a way to free themselves. She looked over at Georgia.

"Give me your necklace."

"What?" she said letting go of the package with her new dress to touch the beads around her neck. "What do you want—"

"The necklace, hurry."

Georgia pulled it over her head and handed it to her. The beads were large and brightly colored, catching the dying light of the early spring day. Molly put the necklace in her jacket pocket and pulled hard, breaking the beads apart, then she moved to the stock trailer door and began feeding the beads out the back.

"Seriously?" Georgia said joining her there.

"Well, we don't have any bread crumbs."

The insurance rep seemed to shake herself out of the trance she'd been in over their abduction. "Do you really think that's going to help?" she asked as she watched her necklace go, the beads bouncing on the quickly disappearing highway as the truck began to slow.

"Sorry about your date," Molly said seeing her friend's expression.

"Silly huh. We're probably about to die and I'm thinking about how much I paid for a dress I'll probably never get to wear."

They were thrown together as the truck turned and the stock trailer swayed before it bounced along the bumpy dirt road.

"Any idea where we are?" Georgia asked.

"No." Molly was busy tossing beads out at intervals. She was almost out of beads and thinking it really had been a dumb idea. No one was looking for them. The sheriff had made it clear that she wouldn't be going with him tonight. How long before the deputy thought he'd been stood up and went home? Would he realize Georgia hadn't stood him up? Would he come looking for her? Doubtful since they hadn't told anyone where they were going.

She tried not to dwell on that as the truck slowed again and turned. She tossed the last couple of beads out and said a silent oath as the truck turned yet again before pulling to a rattling stop.

Chapter Twenty-Three

"I just saw the damnedest thing," the caller said. "Could have been a stunt. You know young people these days. But I swear, the two women looked scared and those two wearing the masks—"

The sheriff got the gist from the caller, then asked about the truck and stock trailer and which direction it had gone. A quick call to Ash at the hotel and he had a pretty good idea who the two women had been.

"They went into Eureka shopping," Ash told him. "Nope, haven't seen them since."

The clothing stores were closed by the time Brandt reached Eureka. He feared he would have to call the shop owners and clerks and that would take valuable time. As it was, he had no idea how long the women had been missing, but he could feel the clock ticking. He had to get them. He could feel the urgency making his fears rise with each second.

Fortunately, he got lucky. He found Molly's

rental car parked in front of one of the closed shops just down the street.

"They were here," the owner told him when he called. "The one couldn't make up her mind. I sent her down the street to Marigold's place."

"Did you notice anyone hanging around or watching the two of them?"

"Sorry, I was busy with the picky one. Didn't have time to look around."

He thanked her and tried Marigold next. Her shop was only a half block away. The women would have walked to it.

Marigold hadn't been working today but gave him her salesclerk's number. Tina answered on the fourth ring. He could hear the television in the background and children's voices along with the clatter of dishes. He'd called right at supper time. He quickly asked about the two women, not surprised that Tina remembered them.

"It took a while, but I found the perfect dress for the one."

"Where was the other one?"

"She went outside to sit on the bench in front, said her feet were killing her." Tina chuckled. "I think her friend had dragged her to every store in town. As it was, I was late closing."

He asked about anyone hanging around, anyone paying a lot of attention to them and got the same answer. "Did you see them leave?"

"I walked them to the door and locked up." He

heard her hesitate. "I saw them start to cross the street when a truck and stock trailer pulled up and almost hit them. I shut off the lights and left by the back way. I didn't see them again."

"You didn't happen to recognize the truck and stock trailer by any chance or see which way it was headed, did you?"

AS THE TRUCK engine shut down, Molly heard the two kidnappers get out. She braced herself, watching the rear door of the stock trailer, terrified of what happened next. She couldn't see any lights in the semidarkness or tell where they had stopped. For all she knew, it could be in the middle of nowhere.

She realized she'd been waiting for some time. The two hadn't come back for them. She looked over at Georgia who was hugging herself and the package with her dress inside.

Neither of them said a word, both apparently listening. Molly picked up the sound of male voices. One male's voice was louder than the other one.

"What the hell were you thinking?"

"He said he wanted her gone. They were together. What else could we do but bring them both?"

The louder one swore. She heard a door slam and looked over at Georgia. Just as she'd feared, this was about her. "I'm sorry."

"I'm sorry about earlier," Georgia said. "Crying

over a date. The thing is…" Her voice broke. "I might as well admit it, since I'm about to die…" Before Molly could correct her, she rushed on. "I haven't been on a date in a very long time. I feel like all I do is work for that damn insurance company night and day and they don't appreciate me in the least."

"If you don't make your date tonight, you will tomorrow."

Georgia laughed. "Are you always such a Pollyanna?"

Molly leaned toward her friend and hugged her. "No one goes on real dates anymore so I'm happy for you. We're a generation so busy we have to meet men online."

"Except now I've been abducted and am never going to meet anyone," Georgia said. "It's been so long since I've met someone…nice, safe. I could be serious about a man like Jaden Montgomery."

Molly nodded, thinking of the sheriff. "I know how you feel. I'm really sorry," she said again thinking how grateful she was for her new friend. "You heard what they said. They only wanted to kidnap me."

Georgia waved it away. "I'm in this as deep as you are. I was the one who insisted you go shopping with me." They both fell silent for a few moments.

Molly felt a start as realization hit her. "Exactly. How did they know we were in town?"

"We went to every shop that sold dresses."

She shook her head.

"Someone was watching the hotel?" Georgia suggested.

Molly thought of Irma's earlier visit. She had to have come through the lobby when Ash wasn't at his post. But if anything, Irma had seemed to want to protect Molly. But if not Irma, then who had seen them both leave?

Everyone in Fortune Creek, she thought with a curse. But maybe someone else as well.

"How are we going to get out of this?" Georgia asked. "I should have my gun in my coat pocket." She began going through her coat pockets, pulling out tissues, coins, lip gloss.

"You have a gun?"

"I never go anywhere without it—except today to go shopping. Don't look so surprised. I checked it at the airport."

"A weapon of some kind might be nice," Molly agreed, though surprised that Georgia carried a gun usually. She checked her own pockets. Empty except for a piece of folded-up paper. Frowning, she realized that she didn't recognize it. In the dying light, she unfolded it and tried to make out what was written on it.

"What's that?" Georgia asked.

"A note." At second glance, she saw it had been written on a page from a Bible. She held it up to the light coming through the cracks in the stock trailer. Someone had circled "An eye for an eye." Written in tiny painful-looking script were the words, *Seth's killer heading for hell*.

A shock wave moved through her. "Irma must have slipped this into my coat pocket when she came to visit me earlier today. My coat was lying on the bed next to where she sat down."

She handed it to Georgia who read the note and said, "Old-time vengeance," and handed it back. Somewhere in the distance a door slammed. "We could use a little of that right now."

Molly could hear someone coming. She and Georgia hadn't had a chance earlier to put up much of a fight. It sounded like they were still outnumbered badly. "I think we should go along with them—until we know what's going on."

Georgia didn't answer as they heard the driver's side door of the truck open followed by the passenger side as two people climbed into the cab. Their abductors? The engine roared and moments later, they were moving again.

Molly felt her heart drop, terrified as to where they were taking them now and what they planned to do with them.

IRMA HEARD CECIL come into the house. She could tell by his heavy step that he was in one of his moods. She'd heard Gage's boys return from town. She knew the sound of each old vehicle they owned. From her kitchen even with pots boiling, she had listened for years to the day-to-day running of this ranch.

She knew she'd been waiting for the sound of her husband's old pickup, afraid of where he might have gone. But apparently he'd just been making himself scarce. Cecil thought he could hide the truth from her even after all these years. One look at him and she knew.

Out of the corner of her eye, Irma saw him pull out a chair at the table and drop into it. She didn't turn around. After spending years with this man, she had no illusions. She thought about what she would tell the mortician to write in his obituary. Cecil Crandell loved the land and his family. He would have done anything for them. Even kill to protect them.

She put down the spoon she'd been stirring their dinner with and, wiping her hands on her apron, turned to look at him. He sat, shoulders hunched, head down, looking like a kicked dog.

Irma took a breath and let it out, her heart pounding so hard it shook her entire body. She could feel the years in her bones, forcing her to remember all the times he'd come into her kitchen with bad news.

"What have you done, Cecil?"

THE SHERIFF DROVE FAST. There was no traffic this time of the evening, let alone this early in the year on this backroad so he didn't need lights and siren.

He hadn't gone far when his headlights began to pick up something shiny in the road.

He saw one small flash of light, then another and another. What the heck? He kept going until he reached the turnoff that would take him into the Crandell Ranch via the back way. As he started to turn, he saw another of the shiny objects in the road ahead.

Pulling up, he opened his door and picked up one. It appeared to be a large bead, brightly colored and made of clear plastic. He'd seen it before, he thought as he slammed the door and hit the gas. Georgia was wearing a necklace just like this the last time he saw her. Ahead more of the beads caught in his headlights.

Brandt shook his head, thinking about the two women locked in a stock trailer, purposely leaving him a trail to follow?

As he came in the back way to the Crandell house, the bead trail stopped. In his headlights, what the sheriff didn't see was a truck and stock trailer, he realized, his heart dropping.

Ahead, he saw a large figure step into the road, a shotgun in his hands. As Brandt roared toward the figure, he put on his lights and siren.

The man didn't move. Instead, the man raised the shotgun.

THE TRUCK PULLING the stock trailer stopped abruptly. Molly had felt every bump on the narrow road, then the wider gravel road. She'd been surprised when the truck had pulled onto pavement.

"Where are they taking us?" Georgia whispered, her tone sounding tight and as frightened as Molly felt.

She didn't answer, but she suspected it wouldn't be good. That was why the paved road had worried her. How far were they going?

The truck slowed, then came to a stop. Molly could see light through the crack of the stock trailer. This time, the driver didn't cut the truck engine and the two of them exited the vehicle.

She and Georgia shared a look as the back of the stock trailer was flung open. "Get out!" the larger of the two ordered. Both were wearing their masks but were no longer brandishing weapons. From the size of them, Molly was sure they were both males although their voices were muffled by the masks.

It took a moment for them to rise. Once on their feet though, they moved to the door. One of the kidnappers helped Molly down. The other grabbed Georgia and pulled her to the pavement.

Looking around, Molly realized that they were back where they'd started—in downtown Eureka. The shops had closed and there was little light on the streets.

"Get out of here!" the larger of the two said as they shoved their purses at them. "Get out of town. No one wants you here." With that the kidnapper shoved past Molly to return to the driver's side of the truck.

"Sorry," the other said, his voice sounding hoarse. He hesitated as if there was more he wanted to say before hurrying around to the passenger-side door. The engine revved and the truck and stock trailer roared away.

"What was that about?" Georgia said, sounding as breathless as Molly felt.

"They weren't supposed to take us," Molly said, still shaken. The street was empty, the darkness around it intense. "Let's go." She was digging into her purse for her keys. "You can still make your date."

THE SHERIFF HIT the brakes just yards from Gage Crandell standing in the road, the man pointing the shotgun directly as his windshield. He was reaching for his weapon, when Cecil Crandell stepped out of the shadows to grab the shotgun away from his son.

In the headlights, he watched the two arguing before Cecil headed toward the patrol SUV and Brandt. Cecil looked older in the harsh light. He reached the sheriff's side window, the shotgun dangling awkwardly from his left hand.

Brandt whirred down his window; his other hand was on his weapon. "What's going on?"

"I killed him," Cecil said, his gravelly voice heavy with emotion. "I killed my son, Seth."

The sheriff looked out his windshield. Gage still stood in the center of the road, head down. Behind him a smaller figure emerged from the shadows. Irma.

"Where are your grandsons?" Brandt asked.

"Coming back from town, alone." They met gazes in the ambient light.

"The women all right?" Cecil nodded. "I'm going to get out now," he told the older man. "I need you to put down the shotgun."

Cecil seemed to hesitate before he threw the shotgun away behind him. It disappeared in the darkness as the elderly man stepped back to let the sheriff exit the vehicle.

Brandt felt the hair stand up on the back of his neck as he watched both Gage and his mother out of the corner of his eye. Neither moved as he put the cuffs on Cecil. After reading him his rights he checked to make sure he didn't have another weapon on him, then opened the back of the patrol SUV and helped Cecil inside.

As he closed the door, he saw that Irma had faded back into the dark. Gage hadn't moved. He tried Molly's number, hoping to hell the old man was telling the truth. It rang three times, his heart pounding as if it was an eternity before she picked up. "Are you okay now?"

"Yes. You know what happened?"

"Yes. Where are you?"

"Georgia and I are headed back to Fortune Creek."

"Good, I'll see you there later. We can talk then," he said as he climbed behind the wheel. He felt a wave of relief wash over him. She sounded shaken, but all right. His heart seemed to slow a little. He'd been so afraid something horrible had happened to her because of all this.

With Gage still standing in the road, Brandt had to back up to turn around. As he headed out the back way from the ranch, he saw more of the beads lying in the road. They shone in his headlights like diamonds. He shook his head, wondering whose idea it had been to try to leave a trail for him to follow.

Fortunately, he'd had a pretty good idea of who had taken the two women after the shop owner had described the truck and stock trailer—and the direction it had headed out of town.

He glanced in his rearview mirror. Cecil was leaning back in the seat, eyes closed. Beyond him through the back window, his son had dropped to his knees in the middle of the road. Irma was nowhere in sight.

Chapter Twenty-Four

It had taken a while to book Cecil and get him into a cell. He'd refused to make a statement other than to say that he'd killed Seth. Brandt had him sign the confession. Cecil had declined to call anyone, including a lawyer.

"What about your son's puppet, Rowdy?" he asked.

Cecil shook his head. That was all. Either he didn't take Rowdy or he had and had since disposed of the puppet.

Brandt had a lot of questions but few answers. Cecil had confessed. Now it was up to the prosecuting attorney to take it from there.

He was anxious to see Molly and get a statement from her, although he had known who had taken her and Georgia on a ride out to the ranch. The question was whether or not the women wanted to press charges.

As he opened the hotel door, his deputy and Georgia appeared to be on their way out. Georgia was all dressed up and so was Jaden. He raised a brow. "I had hoped to take your statement," he said to Georgia.

"Molly can fill you in," she said smiling. "I have a date."

He nodded grinning as he saw that she at least hadn't been too horribly affected by the kidnapping in the stock trailer. "Come by my office tomorrow." As the two left, he heard Jaden ask, "What was that about?"

Georgia's response had been. "It's a long harrowing story. I'll tell you sometime."

He climbed the stairs to Molly's room and knocked. When she opened the door, he caught the sweet scent of her fresh from the bath. Her hair was still damp. She looked so damned good. All he could think was that he was so glad she was all right.

Brandt couldn't help himself. He reached for her and to his surprise, she stepped into his arms. He held her for a long moment, his cheek pressed to her hair, breathing her in, not wanting to let her go.

As he drew back, he looked into her face and felt the impact of his next words. Once he voiced them, she would be leaving. "Cecil Crandell confessed to killing your father. It's over."

She nodded as if not surprised. Her eyes filled with tears. "We don't know why he killed him?"

Brandt shook his head. "Maybe it will come out if it goes to trial."

"Yes, I forgot that there could be a trial," she said as she stepped out of his arms and moved to the hotel window, her back to him. "It will be held here?"

"Probably down in Kalispell."

"What will happen to Cecil?" she asked.

"It could depend. Given his age..."

She turned then to look at him. "Are you saying he might not go to prison?"

"He's confessed to murder. He'd have to go before a judge who can pronounce a sentence. It might not go to trial. Either way, he will probably die behind bars."

She shook her head, her face contorting as she fought her emotions.

"I'm so sorry, Molly," he said as he moved to her. He took her shoulders in his hands. "I wish there was more I could do."

She looked up at him, then whispered, "I think I need some time alone."

He let go of her and took a step back. "Of course. I will need you to stop by my office before you leave town to make a statement about what happened earlier. You have the option of pressing charges."

"I won't be pressing charges," she said.

He nodded, then stepped to the door and stopped. Turning, he asked, "Whose idea was it to drop the beads?"

Her smile couldn't hide the pain he saw etched there, but still his heart did a little bounce. "Mine."

He smiled. "I knew it. Quick thinking."

AFTER THE SHERIFF LEFT, Molly burst into tears. It felt as if she'd been holding back everything, like a dam that now had broken, letting it all out. The pain threatened to overwhelm her. For years she'd said that she hated her father for what he'd done to her. She had wanted his love so badly and blamed him when she didn't get it.

She'd known he was dead, but it hadn't hit home until Cecil had confessed to killing him. Like the sheriff had said, it was over.

She thought about the one chance she'd had to talk to her father when he'd sent her a note that night after his show. Foolishly, she'd wadded it up and thrown it away. If only she could rewind to that night. If only she could have spent a little time with him. Maybe he would have tried to explain.

More than likely wouldn't have, but it still broke her heart that she hadn't even tried to talk to him while he was alive. As May had said, Seth Crandell had demons that followed him his whole life. They'd caught up with him here in Fortune Creek, here in this hotel. Not even changing his name and hiding behind Rowdy could save him. Had he just been counting down the days before he returned here to his fate?

She cried until she was exhausted. She thought

about when he'd left her and her mother. She'd cried then too, always hoping he would come back. Finally she wiped her eyes. She'd cried her last tears for her father.

Sitting up, she then climbed out of the bed and went to the window again. She'd never seen so many stars. The pines looked black in the darkness. There was nothing keeping her here now. She wouldn't stay around to see what happened to Cecil. She couldn't think of him as her grandfather.

What would happen to Irma? She had her son Gage and his sons and their wives. But Molly wondered if they would provide her any comfort. Somehow she doubted it. Whether she hated Cecil for what he'd done or not, his being gone had to leave a huge hole in Irma's life. All those decades married...

Molly couldn't imagine it. Or at least she couldn't before coming here. She'd never wanted to plant roots. Lately she'd been feeling as if she'd already spent too much time in her job, in New York.

She thought about the sheriff and felt herself smile. She wished she was more like Georgia. But the last thing she wanted was a fling with the cowboy sheriff. Something warned her that she wouldn't be able to walk away unharmed if she did. Best leave the man to his life, no matter where the wind took her.

After getting undressed, she crawled into bed.

She'd told herself that she wouldn't be able to sleep. But she must have drifted off because shortly before midnight, she was startled awake to pounding on her door.

The last part of Rowdy's song he'd been singing in her dream stopped abruptly. But not quickly enough that she didn't realize that this time, she hadn't dreamt it—let alone imagined it.

The thought made her turn on the light and look around the room as if she expected to see her father and Rowdy sitting in the chair by the window watching her.

Whoever was at the door was also not part of a dream, she realized as the pounding started up again.

She felt thrown off-balance by all of it as she grabbed her robe and called out, "Who is it?"

THE SHERIFF HAD done some paperwork before going up to his apartment over what locals referred to as the "cop shop." He wasn't hungry. He wasn't even that tired. After opening his bedroom window, he crawled out onto the roof and sat down.

From here he could see the entire town, not that that was anything to boast about—even in the moonlight. He looked across to the hotel. In the summer, he'd often come up here while the town dozed. He would crack open a beer and count his blessings or curse the latest fool thing he'd done.

Tonight he realized that he'd done it again. He'd fallen for a woman he couldn't have. Even as he thought it, he bemoaned the fact that he hadn't even tried to kiss her. The thought made him laugh softly on the nighttime spring breeze.

They'd both known what would have happened if he had kissed her. Molly was no fool. He, on the other hand...

A thought careened past. He grabbed hold of it, sitting up a little straighter. Tomorrow he would have to go out to the Crandell Ranch and talk to Irma, Gage and his sons and daughters-in-law. Was it possible one of them knew what Cecil had done with Rowdy the Rodeo Cowboy?

Maybe more important, was it possible that they knew more about the murder? He was reminded that Gage's fingerprints had been found in Clay Wheaton's pickup. But so were Cecil's and he'd confessed.

Earlier he'd gotten an anonymous tip that had led him to the murder weapon. The gun was now with forensics in Kalispell. Had the tip come from one of Cecil's relatives? Hard to say. He was pretty sure that Gage's sons had kidnapped Molly and Georgia earlier. Just as he was pretty sure the women wouldn't want to press charges. Cecil had his reasons for confessing and not wanting a lawyer or a trial. Once he was sentenced by a judge, his family could begin the healing process, Brandt thought.

Things were typing up neatly. Maybe too neatly. Wasn't that what was bothering him?

From his perch, he saw Jaden bring back his date. The two kissed and parted; Jaden drove back to his house in the direction he'd come from. Georgia had disappeared inside the hotel, only stopping for a moment, to wave goodbye to the deputy before he drove off.

Would she leave without Rowdy being found? What choice did she have? As annoyed with Molly as he'd been originally about her single-mindedness about Rowdy, he wished he could find the dummy for her before she left.

Even as he tried to tell himself that the murder was solved and he could relax, he couldn't help the feeling that this had been too easy. Or maybe it was that something was niggling at him, but he couldn't put his finger on it. Tomorrow, he'd sort it out, he told himself as he climbed back into his bedroom window. He took one last glance over at the hotel where he hoped Molly was now asleep and then closed the window and pulled the shade.

"WHO IS IT?" Molly asked again, this time in a less sleepy croak as she approached the door.

"Me. I have to talk to you."

She groaned at the sound of Georgia's voice. Was she really up to listening to every detail of the date? What time was it anyway?

"I was sleeping," she said as she opened the door and Georgia rushed in.

"I just heard that Cecil Crandell confessed?" she cried as she looked around the room. "Do you have Rowdy? You didn't destroy him, did you? Please tell me you didn't."

Sleepily, Molly moved back to the bed and sat down trying to wake up. She kept thinking about hearing Rowdy singing. Not in a dream. Not in her imagination. But why would someone want her to think that she'd heard Rowdy singing? The same way they'd duped the elderly couple who'd been in a room nearby the night her father died?

"I don't know anything about Rowdy," she said seeing that Georgia was waiting for an answer.

"But if Clay's father confessed…?"

"You'll have to ask the sheriff in the morning," Molly said and mentally kicked herself even as she asked it, "How was your date?" But she needed to get her wits about her, and she couldn't with her new friend here.

Georgia plopped down on the bed beside her, throwing herself back to stare up at the ceiling. "It was amazing just as I'd known it would be."

Molly half listened in between falling asleep sitting up. "Sounds perfect."

"It was."

"Are you still leaving Fortune Creek?" Georgia was quiet for a little too long. Molly lay back and looked over at her. "You aren't seriously thinking of staying."

Her friend wiped away a tear as she shook her head. "Stay somewhere because of a man? Please! I've done that before. Good thing I got a job within the same insurance company because the guy dumped me a few months later. Of course I'm leaving. As amazing as the date and Jaden are, I have to go home." Georgia sat up. "The sheriff really didn't say anything about Rowdy?"

"Sorry, I forgot to ask."

"Does that mean you don't want to destroy Rowdy?"

Molly thought about it for a moment as she too sat up. "I guess not."

"I'd ask what changed your mind, but I'm just glad. Sorry about your dad though."

She nodded. "Thanks."

"Looks like you've worked through some of your issues," Georgia said.

"I'm still a work in progress. I wanted to tell you. If Rowdy isn't found, I don't want the insurance money. If you don't have to pay out, you should be able to keep your job, right?"

"Are you serious?" Georgia was staring at her. "You'd turn down a million dollars?"

Molly nodded. "I can sign something or talk to your boss. Just let me know what you need."

"Wow, that is so nice of you. But I can handle it. I'm just surprised."

She shrugged. "I have everything I need."

Her friend's eyes widened. "The sheriff?"

"No." She looked away. "But it would have been nice."

Georgia laughed. "Nice? I hope it would have been a whole lot better than that. Listen, if you ever get to my part of the country, give me a call. We'll go have a drink together. My treat."

Molly leaned over to hug her. "I'll do that. But only if you will now let me get some sleep."

Her friend rose chuckling. "Goodnight. I'll lock the door behind me. Go to bed. It's late."

Molly climbed back under the covers. Images of the sheriff kept popping up. If it wasn't so late, she would have called him. He'd believe her about the singing, wouldn't he?

She had just nodded off when she heard a sound that made her eyelids fly open. She lay perfectly still for a few moments before she looked toward the door—and the sheet of hotel stationery folded neatly in half illuminated by moonlight shining through the window onto the floor.

Molly started to reach for her phone but stopped herself. After rising from the bed, she padded across the floor and used her big toe to unfold the note.

Her heart began to pound wildly as she read: *If you ever want to see Rowdy the Rodeo Cowboy again, you will meet me* now. *I'll give you twenty minutes. If you don't show alone, I'll destroy the dummy. Meet me by the big rock you can see from your hotel window.*

The note was nothing like the other ones and for a moment she didn't trust that it was real. She definitely knew the large rock. She'd stared out at it enough times.

But go now? In the middle of the night? Not to meet a killer, she told herself. Cecil had confessed. If she got Rowdy back, then Georgia could definitely keep her job.

Even as she thought it, Molly knew it was more than that. She wanted to get Rowdy back for her father. She liked the idea of Rowdy the Rodeo Cowboy being in a museum and thought her father would too. It was wrong for whoever had taken him to keep him—let alone destroy him.

She hurriedly dressed, telling herself she should call the sheriff. But then whoever had Rowdy might destroy him. She pulled her phone from her purse, telling herself that she could call him if she got into trouble. She didn't have much time, she thought as she headed out the fire escape exit.

Chapter Twenty-Five

Brandt bolted upright in bed. Something was wrong. It took him a moment to remember the thought that had awakened him so abruptly. After swinging his legs over the side of the bed, he rose and quickly pulled on his jeans.

He realized that he'd fallen asleep for longer than he'd thought. Moonlight shimmered over the tops of the pines as he rushed downstairs to his office muttering to himself, "Where did I put that?" It took a good twenty minutes before he found what he was looking for. He'd made a copy of the note Clay Wheaton had left on his hotel room bureau top.

The photocopy still showed the ink spots from the leaky pen the ventriloquist had used along with the names and numbers of the two calls he'd wanted made in case of an emergency.

Dropping into his office chair, he called the second number and listened to the recorded message telling him that the insurance company office was closed. He hadn't remembered the name of the company, but now that he had it, he called their New York office, which should have just opened since it was two hours earlier there.

Waiting for the call to be answered, he mentally kicked himself for not doing this sooner. He kept telling himself he was wrong as he listened to it ring. He wanted to be wrong. But something had been bothering him and had finally awoken him with a start as he realized what he might have overlooked.

"Hello," a woman said as she answered. She rattled off the name of the insurance company. "How can we help you?"

He quickly told her who he was and what he needed. "It's a matter of life and death." He gave her his identification information and explained what he needed.

"This is highly unusual. Let me see what I can do. Please hold."

The wait seemed interminable before she came back on the line. "I'm sorry, but I had to check your credentials. You're at the sheriff's office now? I will call you back."

"Please hurry." Even as he told himself that Molly would be in bed sound asleep at this hour, he couldn't help the urgency he felt and the worry that he might be too late. He'd thought about calling her, waking her up and then what? Telling her about the crazy theory he had and to keep her door locked and not let anyone in?

The office phone rang. He quickly answered it. "Sheriff Brandt Parker."

"I have that information you called about." He listened, his heart dropping. From the start of this investigation, it had been about Rowdy. It had always been about Rowdy. He'd been such a fool. He was busy looking for a murderer, thinking the dummy had nothing to do with it.

He hung up and quickly called Molly as he hurried upstairs to finish dressing. His pulse quickened as the call went straight to voicemail. She must have turned off her phone. Swearing, he headed for the hotel at a dead run.

THE WOODS WERE DARK, shadows lurking under the thick pine branches. Rays from the moon fingered through the boughs and bathed the top of the huge rock in moonlight. Through the branches, Molly kept getting glimpses of the rock, assuring her she was headed in the right direction.

She gripped her phone in her hand. She knew she shouldn't be out here alone. But then again, she wasn't alone. Someone was waiting for her.

As she walked, she tried to make sense of everything that had happened. Did it surprise her that Cecil had confessed to killing her father? From what she'd seen, she thought the rancher certainly was angry enough to do it.

In her memory, she called up the image of him standing on his porch, the shotgun in his hand.

As she did, she recalled something that made her frown. His hands had shaken. She'd blamed it on his fury at her and the sheriff being on his property.

His hands had been shaking still when she'd crossed the porch right next to him and gone in the house to talk to Irma. She'd only noticed out of the corner of her eye. The shotgun leaning against the side of the house. Cecil trying to hide the trembling fingers of his hands. Trying to hide his weakness.

Molly felt a start and almost stumbled into a tree limb. His fingers were clawlike. Arthritis? Would he even have been able to fire the shotgun?

Her mind leaped to the ransom notes. There was no way he could have written them. Someone had tried hard to make it look as if he had though, or that they had been written by someone trying to conceal their real handwriting, but it hadn't been Cecil Crandell.

Molly stopped. The rock was only a few dozen yards ahead. The person waiting would have heard her approach. They would be ready for her.

But who was waiting for her?

THE SHERIFF GRABBED the spare key for Molly's room as well as Georgia's from behind the hotel desk. He would try to rouse Molly by pounding on her door, but if that didn't work, he was going rogue.

She must have turned off her phone since it had gone straight to voicemail, he told himself as he charged up the stairs to the fourth floor and down the hall to pound on her door. No answer. His heart was thundering as he inserted the key, knowing he was breaking the law. But if he hadn't gotten the second key from downstairs, he would have broken down the door, screw the consequences.

The door swung open. In the shaft of moonlight coming through the window, he saw at once that the bed was empty. He rushed in. "Molly?"

Within in seconds, he knew with certainty that she wasn't here. As he started to head for Georgia's room, he saw the sheet of hotel stationery lying on the table by the door. He swore as he read it, wondering how much of a head start she'd had.

At the window, he looked out at the huge rock visible beyond the pines. Why would she go alone? Because she was determined to see this through to the end. Because she didn't trust him? Or because this was something she wanted to do on her own?

He swore and quickly left the room and went to Georgia's. He knew before he opened the door that she was gone.

Out the window, a light flashed on near the large rock. Brandt took off at top speed. He had to get to Molly before it was too late.

ALL MOLLY'S INSTINCTS told her to turn around and run. But if she ever wanted to know the truth... Whoever was waiting for her turned on a flashlight. It went off quickly, but she knew now where the person was—on the dark side of the huge rock.

She took a step forward then another. The cold air was filled with the scent of pine and the creek nearby. A breeze moaned softly in the tops of the pine boughs as she walked toward the rock on the soft bed of dried needles.

She hadn't gone far when the trees opened to a small meadow next to the rock. Standing at the edge of the trees, she saw him waiting for her. She was startled for a moment because of his resemblance to Cecil, and to her own father. He was a large man, like his father and brother.

"Did you bring the money?" Gage asked.

She patted her purse. There was a couple hundred dollars inside it. She hoped he wouldn't demand to see the money first. She'd come here wanting answers. She'd love to save Rowdy for her father, but mostly, she wanted to know who killed him. The theory was that whoever killed the ventriloquist had Rowdy.

"Where's Rowdy?"

Gage Crandell stepped to one side revealing Rowdy's case resting against the base of the rock.

"Please open it."

Gage scoffed. "You're not very trusting, you big-city types." He opened the case and she got a glimpse of Rowdy's painted face before he snapped it closed again.

"If your father killed mine, then how is it that you have Rowdy?" she asked staying where she stood, a half dozen yards away.

"How do you think?"

"You're going to let your father take the fall for this?"

Gage laughed. "Believe me, he's safer in prison. When my mother finds out that he confessed to killing Seth, her favorite son, he's a dead man. She already blames him for not telling her that Seth was in the area, let alone for seeing her son without telling her. There is no happy ending here."

Molly didn't know what to say. This man standing before her was her blood. That alone was a chilling thought.

"You just don't get it," Gage said taking a step toward her. "My father and I went to the hotel that night to kill Seth. I'd left a book stuck in the fire escape door so we could get in. He hadn't wanted me to come with him. I jumped into his truck as he started to leave."

"You knew he was going to the hotel to kill your brother?"

He huffed. "He had his gun with the silencer on it. Yeah, I knew. It had been building up ever since we'd gone to the hotel the first time to see Seth. My old man had killed Seth in his heart, in his mind, in his very soul. I wanted him to do it. That's why I went along."

Molly felt sick to her stomach listening to this.

"But he couldn't do it. Even when he had Seth down on his knees waiting for the bullet to enter the back of his head, my father couldn't do it." He sounded both disappointed and disgusted. "I watched from down the hall as he dropped the gun and left. Maybe he was hoping Seth would take his own life."

She had trouble finding her voice as she realized that she had done what Brandt had feared— she'd met a killer in the woods all alone. "What did you do?" Her voice came out a whisper.

"I left the book in the door and followed my father down the fire escape. He was driving off, leaving me there as if he'd forgotten me. Nothing unusual about that. I was the forgotten son, the one who'd gotten trapped on the ranch after the only two sons my parents ever cared about were dead and gone."

Molly heard the bitterness in his voice. She swallowed knowing in her heart what happened next. "You went back to your brother's room."

Gage nodded, looking as if he was reliving that night. "Seth had made it so easy for my father. He wanted him to kill him, or maybe he was already dead, you know, maybe sending him away like he had, had already killed Seth and that's why he changed his name, that's why he had that silly doll that talked for him."

"You went back and killed him."

He looked at her and blinked. "No. When I reached his room, Seth was already dead. The gun was gone. I just took the pen and some paper."

She stared at him. Was he telling the truth? "What about Rowdy?"

"My father had the case when he left. Not sure what he planned to do with it, not sure he even knew. Destroy it probably. But when he reached the bottom of the fire escape stairs, he just threw the case into the bushes. I retrieved it, hiding it until I went back upstairs to finish what he'd started. Maybe I planned to kill Seth—I don't know. But I didn't have to. I took his pickup keys and left. I got my son Cliff to follow me back to Fortune Creek to leave the pickup behind the hotel."

"If any of this is true, then who killed your brother?"

"I don't know. But I need that five thousand to be able to leave, to buy my freedom. This is my chance to escape the prison my brothers left me in. I was forced to stay here, be the good, loyal, hardworking rancher's son who couldn't abandon his parents especially after they'd lost their other sons. Both Ty and Seth are now free. I'm tired of envying them for getting away from this life. I want to be free too."

"That works out well then," said a voice from the trees behind Molly an instant before she heard the gunshot and saw Gage grab his chest and slowly slump to the ground next to Rowdy's case.

BRANDT'S HEART DROPPED to his boots at the sound of the gunshot. He'd been moving quickly through the pines, the large rock in sight. He'd put it all together—but not fast enough. Maybe not fast enough to save Molly. His chest contracted at the thought, making it hard to breathe.

The rock was not far now. He could hear voices. But a sound closer made him stumble. Someone was directly behind him.

The blow seemed to come from out of nowhere. He caught only a flash of movement. He went down hard in the dried pine needles. Then in a blink there was nothing but blackness.

GEORGIA STEPPED FROM the darkness of the trees into the moonlight.

Molly stared, stunned to see the gun in her hand now pointed at her. "You really did bring a gun."

She smiled. "I told you, I never leave home without it."

"What's going on?" She felt confused by this Georgia holding the gun pointed in her direction.

"You could say that I'm saving you and getting Rowdy back." She tsked. "I thought you were going to tell me when you heard from the person who had the puppet? I trusted you."

Her mind raced, unable to understand what was happening. "You shot Gage."

"Yes, well…you forgot to mention that there'd been a ransom demand for Rowdy. If I hadn't heard about the notes being found under your door, I might have given up and left town without the dummy. But I knew someone had it and if anyone could find it, it would be you or that damned cowboy sheriff. Couldn't leave without knowing where Rowdy was."

Molly still couldn't get her head around what was happening. "Why would you shoot Gage? He was about to give me Rowdy. It would have been over. You would have had the dummy and saved your job."

"Yes, my job that I hate," Georgia said. "When your father came in wanting to ensure Rowdy, I saw a way out. I didn't know some fool was going to murder him and take the dummy. That hadn't been part of the plan. I figured the way Clay Wheaton looked when he came in to sign the paperwork that he didn't have much time left. You still don't get it, do you?"

She didn't. She was still too shocked to make sense of any of it.

"I changed the beneficiary. You were never going to get a million dollars. Your father signed a fake one with you as the beneficiary. I had him sign another page—this one—so when he died and Rowdy didn't turn up, I would collect the insurance."

"But only if you split it with me," came another voice behind Molly, another one she recognized.

BRANDT SURFACED WITH a blinding headache.

He pushed himself up. He could hear voices coming through the trees, his memory returning like a swift kick to his solar plexus. He rose, staggered for a moment, then began to move toward the sound, telling himself that as long as they were talking, Molly might still be alive.

MOLLY TURNED TO see Jessica Woods, the alleged paranormal investigator she'd met at the café. Jessica came out of the trees from the direction of the road out of town. Like Georgia, she was armed. Molly had a sudden flashback of that day in the hotel when she'd thought that the two of them were in league together. It had been such an uncharitable thought that she'd felt bad about it. Now she realized that her instincts had been right. Just too late to do anything about it. Georgia and Jessica had been in this together.

"You were both *pretending* you were looking for Rowdy," she said.

"Oh, we weren't pretending," Georgia said. "We definitely needed Rowdy not to be found before we could get our hands on it and destroy it so we could collect the insurance money. You, Molly, with all your righteous behavior, were the fly in the ointment. Would you really have given up a million dollars to help me?"

"I would have," she said. "You were my friend. I didn't want you to lose your job."

Georgia laughed. "Didn't I tell you, Jess? She's a saint, straight arrow, gullible as all get-out. Her and the cowboy sheriff."

"I see you have your phone," Jessica said. "I wouldn't bother trying to call him. The sheriff won't be coming to save you. I ran into him in the woods. I left him out cold."

Molly's body went limp. She staggered, terrified to think what Jessica had done to him. The phone had been her backup. Now there was no one coming to save either of them. "Was the deputy part of your plan too?" she asked, surprised that her voice sounded almost normal to her ears.

"Jaden?" Georgia laughed. "He was just for amusement and information. I figured he'd know if Rowdy was found and tell me. But he didn't even know about the ransom demands. You and the sheriff kept that bit of information to yourselves."

"We should get moving," Jessica said. "Grab the dummy and let's go. I can finish this up." Georgia moved toward the rock and the case with Rowdy inside. Gage hadn't moved. "Leave the case—that way no one will ever know if the dummy was in there or not."

Finish up? Molly held her breath afraid she already knew what they had planned.

"Sad that your uncle killed you, Molly. But at least you got off a shot that ended his life as well. Jaden will find an unregistered gun lying by each of you with your prints on one and Gage's on the other. Shouldn't have come out here by yourself. Should have called me." Georgia was saying. "When I hear what happened, I'm going to be devastated. We'd become such good friends." Georgia reached down to open Rowdy's case.

Gage's hand shot out. Molly caught the glint of a gun an instant before she heard the shots. Two of them, fired quickly in succession. Georgia went down hard next to Rowdy lying inside his open case. Behind her, Molly heard Jessica swear and instinctively rush forward.

The moment she did, Molly lunged for her and the gun in her hand.

TWO SHOTS ECHOED through the trees. Brandt didn't know how long he'd been out as he struggled to his feet. Too long. He ran toward the rock, terrified of what he would find. As he burst out of the pines, his own weapon drawn, his head pounding, fear gripped him as he took in the sight before him in the moonlight. Near the rock, there was no movement. He could see Gage slumped over, Georgia on the ground in front of Rowdy's case.

At first he didn't see Molly. Everyone seemed to be down. But then he saw movement. Molly and Jessica grappling on the ground. The shine of the gun in Jessica's hand in the moonlight as the two rolled, Jessica coming out on top.

He charged toward them, terrified of taking a shot for fear he would hit Molly and yet at the same time, terrified not to take the shot. The bang of a gunshot was followed by a second one. Both seemed to fill the small meadow, echoing off the large boulder.

For a moment, nothing moved. Brandt blinked. Jessica was still looming over Molly, the gun in her hand. And then Molly wrestled the gun away and Jessica slowly collapsed to the ground beside her.

Brandt rushed to Molly, dropping to his knees next to her, his gun still in his hand as he stared at her in the moonlight. He'd been terrified by all the blood, convinced Jessica had shot her.

"Are you hit?" he cried and felt a drowning wave of relief when she shook her head.

"I got it all," Molly said as he took her in his arms.

It wasn't until hours later after reinforcements had arrived, Gage had been rushed to a hospital and that he and Molly were in his office, that Brandt understood her words. She'd recorded everything on her phone.

Chapter Twenty-Six

Brandt listened to the recording on Molly's phone a second time. It was all there, the truth and not just about Gage, but about Georgia and Jessica. After Molly had told him about hearing Rowdy singing at night, he'd done a search of her room and the one adjoining it on the opposite side as Georgia's.

He'd found the small recorder in the air vent and known only one person could have put it there. He almost had everything he needed to release Cecil from jail—and arrest the person he now believed had killed Clay Wheaton, a.k.a. Seth Crandell.

He just needed proof.

Molly was at the hotel, no doubt packing to leave. He told himself this shouldn't take long as he grabbed his Stetson and drove to Eureka. After everything he'd learned, he thought the prosecutor could make a pretty good case.

The sheriff just needed a few things clarified.

Tom Sherman looked up in surprise at finding Brandt standing in his doorway. "Sheriff," he said as he got to his feet, placing both hands on his desk. For support? Or so Brandt didn't see how nervous he was? "I heard you caught Seth's killer. Congrats."

"Guess you haven't heard the latest." He saw a tick around Tom's mouth. "Cecil Crandell didn't kill him."

"I thought I heard you found his gun?"

"Did through an anonymous tip after Cecil was arrested."

"I should think that would be sufficient to put him away for a long time."

Brandt nodded. "I have crime techs breaking down the weapon as we speak. That's the thing about killers. They just assume they can wipe prints off a gun, but they always miss a spot. All we need is one clear print."

He saw Tom swallow and shift nervously on his feet, waiting. "I suspect the killer was worried there wouldn't be enough evidence against Cecil, even though the man had confessed. Oftentimes people confess to cover for someone else."

"His son Gage," Tom said quickly. "I thought of that myself."

"Gage didn't kill Seth."

"What?"

"I'm going to need your fingerprints, Tom."

The man had the look of someone about to make a run for it. "Why?"

"I'm betting we are going to find Seth's prints

in your SUV. You did meet with him before the night you killed him, didn't you? Did he tell you what happened the night your sister died? Or did he continue to cover for his brother Ty? I'm also betting that you've been watching the hotel, waiting for an opportunity to get what you believed was justice."

"You can't prove—"

"That's just it—I think I can. I forgot to mention," Brandt said. "Seth's small recorder was found. He'd recorded Rowdy's songs on it, probably liked to play them at night. I would imagine that's what the elderly couple a few doors down heard the night Seth died. The night you murdered him, you retrieved the recorder when you heard Ash coming up on the elevator. You sure you didn't leave your fingerprints on the recorder? How about the tape inside?"

"You can't prove anything," Tom said, sounding more confident than he looked.

"Jaden," Brandt said to his deputy who'd been waiting in the hall. "Would you please read Mr. Sherman his rights?"

As the deputy approached him, Tom's expression crumpled. He dropped into his chair. "Someone needed to get justice for Ruby. Your father sure as hell didn't."

"But you killed the wrong man, Tom. Seth wasn't responsible for your sister's death, Ty was. I suspect that's why he killed himself."

Tom's eyes widened. "I want a lawyer."

"I'm sure you have one you can call," Brandt said. "But I'm curious. Why did you leave the recorder in the hotel, set up where you could operate it remotely in the room next to Seth's daughter?" he asked after Jaden had read Tom his rights.

Tom shook his head. "If that ridiculous dummy hadn't been missing, she and the others would have left town and it would have been over. I could have put Ruby to rest, finally after all these years."

"You tried to scare away the wrong person," Brandt said. "All you did was make her more determined to find her father's killer and find Rowdy."

"Rowdy," Tom said with a bark of laughter. "That damned puppet. You're right. Seth and I did meet. He didn't even have the guts to tell me the truth about what happened to my sister. He had the puppet do it. I should have killed them both then."

Brandt watched Jaden lead the man out of his office toward the patrol SUV parked outside thinking what a tragedy it had all been. If Cecil hadn't dropped his gun that night in the ventriloquist's room, maybe Tom never would have picked it up and killed Seth.

The irony was that if Tom had waited, Seth would have died of natural causes and Tom wouldn't be arrested for homicide right now.

Chapter Twenty-Seven

"I don't want you to go."

Molly turned to look at Brandt. She smiled at the handsome cowboy sheriff in the noisy Kalispell airport. It had taken a while before she'd been able to smile after everything that had happened.

Tom Sherman's arrest had rocked the county. Tom's fingerprints had been found on the tape recorder cassette as well as a partial on the trigger of the gun.

The townfolk of Fortune Creek had been more shocked when it came to Georgia Eden. Like Molly, everyone had liked Georgia. She'd fooled them all, especially Molly.

That was what made it so hard, she thought now as she picked up the case with Rowdy safely inside. Her suitcase was already being loaded onto the plane. She'd thought she'd found a friend.

"I have a feeling that we'll see each other again," she said meeting Brandt's gaze.

"Not soon enough to suit me," he said stepping

to her. His kiss was pure honey, his hand cupping her neck warm and reassuring. "You sure about this?" he asked as he drew back from the kiss.

"I want to personally deliver Rowdy to the museum," she said. At least that part of Georgia's story was true. The money would go to Gage, her uncle who had helped save her life. He was still in the hospital, but doctors said he should make a full recovery.

When he did, Molly wanted him to have the option of leaving the ranch that he'd felt trapped on all these years.

"You know that he probably won't leave," Brandt had said when she'd told him of her plan.

"Probably not since his sons are there, his mother and father. He might not realize how strong those roots are that have held him there," she said. "But I like the idea of Rowdy maybe saving Gage's life since he'd saved Rowdy."

"I never thought you'd really destroy it," Brandt said now, motioning to the case with the Crandell Ranch brand on it.

She smiled, wondering if that was true. "It took my father's murder for me to finally get to know him." She shook her head ruefully. "I wish he knew how sorry I am."

The sheriff scoffed. "You risked your life to save Rowdy and now your father's memory will live on at the museum. I think he knows." He drew her to him as tears welled in her eyes.

As her flight was called, he let go of her. She wiped her eyes. "If you're ever in Fortune Creek again, give me a holler."

ON THE WAY back to Fortune Creek, Brandt stopped by a bookstore and picked up a copy of *East of Eden*. Jaden had remembered it from high school, but Brandt wasn't sure he'd gotten around to actually reading it. Back in those days, rodeoing was all he'd cared about.

It hadn't taken him long to read it once back in Fortune Creek. He'd known how the story would end. Two brothers, one the father's favorite, a deadly rivalry between the two. He thought of Gage Crandell, who would have been fifteen the year Ruby Sheridan died and his brother Seth joined the military and his younger brother Ty killed himself.

Brandt had wondered if there was a reason *East of Eden* was the book stuck in the door the night the ventriloquist died. Or had Gage randomly chosen the book?

He'd taken the book by the hospital. "Have you read this?" he asked Gage who shook his head. "I think you might want to. Might make you feel like you weren't alone."

One son loved, one son hated, one son feeling unloved, he'd thought as he'd left the hospital.

Chapter Twenty-Eight

Helen spotted her first. The dispatcher had been getting Ghost a drink when she saw the car pull up out front.

Brandt heard her exclaim in the room outside his office and looked up. Helen, the woman who always said she didn't like dogs, was holding that ball of white fluff that had been rescued from Jessica Woods's pickup.

The sheriff had been planning to take it to the shelter, but Helen wasn't having any of that. She'd scooped up the furball and the two had been inseparable ever since. It had surprised him, but not as much as learning that Jessica really had been a ghost hunter by profession. How she and Georgia had crossed paths was still a mystery.

"Well, I'll be darned," Helen said. "Would you look at that."

He looked past her in time to see Molly standing by what appeared to be a new SUV. He smiled so hard that it hurt his face. She had come back?

For weeks, every time they'd talked, she'd said

she was tying up loose ends. He hadn't pressed her, knowing it would be a mistake. As it was, he couldn't imagine what a woman like her would do in Fortune Creek. Would she even last a week if she did come back?

He'd warned himself not to get his hopes up and yet here she was. He pushed himself up from his desk and walked toward the door. The look on her face was definitely one that said, *And you thought you'd never see me again.*

It was true. Not that he could blame her. They were from two completely different worlds. Murder had thrown them together. That and a dummy named Rowdy the Rodeo Cowboy. But it would take a lot more to keep them together, Brandt thought as he pushed open the sheriff's department door and stepped out into the sunshine. It would take a love strong enough to last forever.

Summer had come to Fortune Creek slowly; after all, this was Montana and only miles from the Canadian border. His father used to joke that the weather kept out the riffraff—until summer.

Today was one of those early summer days when the sky was a blinding blue, the sun a lolling ball of heat, making the pine-covered mountains shimmer with light. People fell in love with Montana in the summer.

"You came back," he said as he stopped on the sidewalk to take her in.

"Couldn't stay away."

He glanced at the SUV. It was packed to the top. "Almost looks like you're moving in."

She grinned. "Don't believe me? How about you come over here, cowboy? I think I have just what will convince you."

"That right?" he asked as he stepped toward her. He had no idea what had brought her back, let alone what might keep her here with him.

But when he reached her, she stepped to him and kissed him.

He felt his heart take off like the bald eagle he'd seen earlier flying across Montana's big sky. It had been free to go anywhere it wanted, but it stayed here in this isolated part of the state—just like him.

Brandt drew back from the kiss to look at her. "What in the hell are you going to do in Fortune Creek?"

"You mean after I marry you? See that building down the street? I want it. I'm going to open a business." He cocked a brow at her. "Don't worry—I'm a financial analyst. I know what I'm doing."

He laughed and pulled her into his arms. "If that was true, you wouldn't be interested in marrying a small-town cowboy sheriff."

"Try me," Molly said and kissed him again.

When their kids asked one day, Brandt planned to tell them that it was a kiss that had done it. Their mother had stolen his heart with one amazing kiss—and the rest would be history.

"Ask the woman to marry you, fool," Helen said from the doorway.

As he pulled back, he saw that half the town had come out into the sunshine. It was true that nothing much ever happened in Fortune Creek, that even the birth of a calf made news.

So he wasn't that surprised that he and Molly were making a stir.

He dropped to one knee right there in the main street and dug out the ring he'd been carrying for months, thinking himself a fool. He looked up blinded by this woman's beauty and strength. "Marry me," he said.

"I thought you would never ask," she joked and then she was in his arms. Some of the people who'd gathered cheered. Some just went back to their business. Helen huffed and took her new dog back inside the sheriff's department.

Brandt wondered how many people would be taking bets on whether the marriage would last. He smiled to himself. He had a good feeling about this. He was putting his money on the two of them.

There was going to be a wedding in Fortune Creek! He couldn't wait to make this woman his wife.

* * * * *